She wanted Elias Garcia. She had wanted him the moment she first saw him. And maybe, just maybe, if she gave in to that hunger, that driving need that had burned in her blood since they had met, she could get on with her life. She could get him out of her system. He took a step closer to her, as if he were thinking the same thing, as if he were fighting the same thing she was feeling, too.

The attraction.

"Elias," she whispered, her heart racing. She needed to step away from him. This was too dangerous.

"I want to kiss you, Adeline. No, scratch that. I'm going to kiss you, Adeline."

Adeline nodded and met him halfway. She was more than willing to get swept away in this moment.

Elias's hands were in her hair as he kissed her, passionate and intense. Just the way she wanted.

Just the way she needed.

All she wanted was the heat, the pleasure and the rush with him.

No. You can't do this.

She pushed him away as the kiss ended. "I can't."

Even though she wanted to.

Dear Reader,

Thank you for picking up a copy of Adeline & Elias's story, *Twin Surprise for the Baby Doctor*.

California is one of my favorite places, so I always get a thrill when I write a book in the sunshine state.

Adeline has been focused on one goal her entire career and that's to work with Dr. Wilder, the best in maternal fetal medicine. Nothing is going to get in her way, not even the sexy new competition, Dr. Elias Garcia.

Elias is bent on proving to his family that he is the best, and getting the coveted fellowship with Dr. Wilder would be a coup. The problem is, a very tempting competitor is standing in his way.

Adeline and Elias are both strong competitors, but after one night of passion, the competition melts away and family is about to be formed.

I hope you enjoy Adeline and Elias's story.

I love hearing from readers, so please drop by my website, www.amyruttan.com, or give me a shout on Twitter @ruttanamy.

With warmest wishes,

Amy Ruttan

TWIN SURPRISE FOR
THE BABY DOCTOR

———

AMY RUTTAN

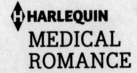

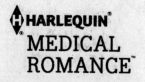

HARLEQUIN®
MEDICAL
ROMANCE™

Recycling programs
for this product may
not exist in your area.

ISBN-13: 978-1-335-40443-5

Twin Surprise for the Baby Doctor

Copyright © 2021 by Amy Ruttan

All rights reserved. No part of this book may be used or reproduced in
any manner whatsoever without written permission except in the case of
brief quotations embodied in critical articles and reviews.

This is a work of fiction. Names, characters, places and incidents
are either the product of the author's imagination or are used fictitiously.
Any resemblance to actual persons, living or dead, businesses,
companies, events or locales is entirely coincidental.

This edition published by arrangement with Harlequin Books S.A.

For questions and comments about the quality of this book,
please contact us at CustomerService@Harlequin.com.

Harlequin Enterprises ULC
22 Adelaide St. West, 40th Floor
Toronto, Ontario M5H 4E3, Canada
www.Harlequin.com

Printed in U.S.A.

Born and raised just outside Toronto, Ontario, **Amy Ruttan** fled the big city to settle down with the country boy of her dreams. After the birth of her second child, Amy was lucky enough to realize her lifelong dream of becoming a romance author. When she's not furiously typing away at her computer, she's mom to three wonderful children, who use her as a personal taxi and chef.

Books by Amy Ruttan

Harlequin Medical Romance

First Response
Pregnant with the Paramedic's Baby

Cinderellas to Royal Brides
Royal Doc's Secret Heir

Hot Greek Docs
A Date with Dr. Moustakas

The Surgeon King's Secret Baby
A Mommy for His Daughter
NY Doc Under the Northern Lights
Carrying the Surgeon's Baby
The Surgeon's Convenient Husband
Baby Bombshell for the Doctor Prince
Reunited with Her Hot-Shot Surgeon
A Reunion, a Wedding, a Family

Visit the Author Profile page
at Harlequin.com for more titles.

For Katherine.
Thank you for your continued support

CHAPTER ONE

TODAY WAS GOING to be a good day.

Adeline could feel it and she couldn't help but smile as she walked the halls of San Diego Mesa Hospital. Dr. Oleson, the last real threat—competition—to the fellowship with the world-renowned maternal-fetal medicine physician, Dr. Wilder, had accepted a position in New York.

There was nothing in her way now.

In a couple of months she'd be the surgeon chosen for one of the most prestigious fellowships on the Western Seaboard.

All her hard work was about to pay off and she couldn't wipe the smile off her face.

"You look happy today, Dr. Turner," Nurse Keeper said, handing her a chart.

"I am. Dr. Oleson took a position in New York." Adeline tried not to squeal. She was bouncing on her heels.

Nurse Keeper cocked an eyebrow. "I didn't know you two were so close that you're so happy he's gone on to a better position."

"We weren't, but you know he and I were the front-runners for the fellowship. He was good, but he was in my way. Now he's not."

Nurse Keeper's lips formed a firm line and Adeline's stomach knotted. Keeper only made that face when there was trouble. The head nurse of the OB-GYN floor could be read like a book. Suddenly her bright sunny day got a little dimmer. Her stomach sank like a rock.

"What?" Adeline asked. "When you make that face…"

"There's a new resident. Fresh from Houston, Texas." Nurse Keeper walked away, and with the shake of her head, Adeline's optimism faded away.

So what? It's a new doctor. They come and go.

Other residents, other surgeons joined the program and they were no competition, but something deep down inside her said that this day had decidedly gotten worse and her instincts weren't usually wrong.

And after medical school and her disastrous first love affair with the wrong man, she'd learned to listen to her instincts, because they were telling her to be wary.

Her positive outlook vaporized, and now she was dreading today and would continue to worry until she met her new competition.

Every new doctor who joined this residency was her competition. It meant everything to her.

It was a way to prove to all those from her first medical school that she was more than just a screwup.

Don't think about that.

Only she couldn't help but think about it.

How falling for and trusting the wrong people had almost cost her her medical career.

It was why she kept people at bay.

Why she didn't trust anyone but herself.

She shook her head, banishing that thought. She wasn't going to let Gregory and her broken heart into her head today.

Not today.

She had to be in the game today.

No one in this program was her friend. She'd learned the hard way not to make friends when it came to her career.

Dr. Wilder was speaking to the new doctor and Adeline could only see his back. He was tall, taller than her, and she was five-foot-nine. She had to guess at six-foot-two, and then he turned around and her heart skipped a beat. She paused and stared, because that's all she could do.

She had never seen such a handsome man before. His dark eyes were twinkling, and his brown hair had haphazard curls. There was a dimpled half smile on his face, and as she stared at him, his gaze landed on her. A zing of electricity passed through her.

Warmth spread up her neck into her cheeks and she hated the fact that she blushed.

She hadn't felt like this in a long time—not since Gregory. She was angry with herself as soon as the thought crossed her mind.

Dr. Wilder turned and looked at her.

"Ah, Dr. Turner. I'd like to introduce you to the doctor who took Dr. Oleson's place. Dr. Adeline Turner, this is Dr. Elias Garcia. He's joining us from Houston."

Dr. Garcia smiled at her again, and his gaze traveled over her in a way that sent another zing of warmth through her. It set her on edge.

"A pleasure to meet you, Dr. Turner." Dr. Garcia held out his hand, and Adeline grudgingly took it because Dr. Wilder was watching.

"Same." That was all she could get out.

Her gut instincts were never wrong, and this time they were telling her this guy was trouble.

Sexy trouble.

And she hated the way he was affecting her, that she was attracted to him.

"Dr. Turner, I'd like you to show Dr. Garcia the ropes today and work on the discharge patients."

Adeline's forced smile disappeared. "Discharge patients? I thought I was helping with consults today?"

Dr. Wilder looked at her coldly. "I can do those. Today you will show Dr. Garcia the hospital and handle discharges."

"Of course." Adeline was disappointed, as she had been looking forward to handling consults on her own for a month.

Now she was babysitting the new member of the team, who was her direct competition.

She was annoyed, but there was nothing she could do about it.

Dr. Wilder nodded and walked away, leaving her standing there with Dr. Garcia.

Alone.

Adeline couldn't say anything at first. She couldn't figure out what to say. She didn't want to say the wrong thing or give him any fodder to use against her.

"Why don't you give me half of the files, and you take the other half?" Dr. Garcia suggested, breaking the silence. "That way I can get to work."

"Pardon?" Adeline asked.

Dr. Garcia crossed his arms and looked irritated. "Look, I don't need a babysitter. I'm here for a fellowship, so if you could hand over the charts, I can get started."

Adeline crossed her arms as well, taking a step closer to Elias. "Well, I'm not a babysitter, but I can tell you that these patients are patients I have a rapport with. You don't understand the procedures at San Diego Mesa Hospital. Until you do, I am the babysitter. So, if you'll follow me, we can start our day."

"Follow you? I'm hardly an intern and you're hardly an attending."

Adeline cocked an eyebrow. "I was an attending for a year in OB-GYN before this position came up, so I am a senior surgeon here."

Elias wanted to smile. He enjoyed a feisty woman. The problem was, this particular feisty woman was his competition.

He'd heard of Dr. Adeline Turner when he was accepted to take Dr. Oleson's spot, and Elias knew she was the one to beat.

In his mind's eye he had had a picture of what to expect, and his expectation didn't match the reality standing in front of him.

Dr. Adeline Turner took his breath away. She was beautiful, and for one fraction of a second, his blood heated in attraction. Then she opened her mouth and it brought him back to earth.

This wasn't some woman he could chat up at a bar.

This woman.

This was the surgeon he had to beat.

She was strong-willed. Obviously smart because she was the one to watch out for. Her blond hair was tied back, and he couldn't help but wonder what it would look like down.

She had dark brown eyes and full pink lips and a pink glow in her cheeks when she got flustered. He was attracted to her, but he'd have to ignore that. He wasn't here to date or get involved with anyone. Even someone as beautiful as Dr. Adeline Turner.

Get control. She's your competition.

Elias had no time for romance. He had no interest in it. He'd opened his heart up a long time ago and it had bitten him in the ass.

Even among his own family, the only person he could rely on was himself.

No one understood him.

He knew only one thing—his career never let him down.

It meant everything to him, and there was no way he was getting involved with his rival.

There was only one position in this fellowship with Dr. Wilder, and it was going to be his.

Elias always succeeded in whatever he set out to do with his career.

His father had never thought it would amount to anything, but this fellowship would prove to his father that he'd finally made it.

Will it?

Elias shook that thought away and stared down at those big, dark brown eyes of Dr. Turner glaring up at him.

"I happened to be a pediatric attending, a specialist in the NICU in Houston. So I guess we're on equal footing."

A strange smirk crossed her face. "We're not

on equal footing. I've been here longer. You're new. So you follow my lead. Got it?"

Elias was annoyed, but he couldn't help but smile.

She was going to be a challenge, but he could handle a challenge.

This was *his* fellowship.

It would be a great coup to have this specialty on his CV. Everyone would come to him.

Everyone except your family.

He dismissed the thought. He didn't want to think about his family or the fact that he hadn't seen them in two years.

That was his own choice.

It had been five years since his now ex-fiancée had left him for his younger brother. Relations with his family had been strained since, and it distracted him. He couldn't focus when he was around them.

That's because you can't stand your dad's dis-appointment.

Elias's stomach twisted. He didn't want to think about it.

All that mattered was his career, and this fellowship would mean he'd be at the top of his game. He could have any job he wanted, anywhere.

And nothing was going to stand in his way.

Not even the beautiful temptation of Dr. Adeline Turner.

* * *

Arrogant jerk.

Adeline grumbled to herself as she walked home from the hospital where she worked. Thankfully, it was still early afternoon and the rush hour traffic, both foot and car, hadn't started in San Diego. There was no one else on the street who would get in her way and possibly become victim to her particularly foul mood.

Which sucked.

Her day had started out so well—another perfect day—until the new resident had shown up. Dr. Elias Garcia. She had been stuck with him all day doing discharges when she should have been running the consult clinic.

She'd been waiting to do that clinic for three months.

And instead she had been babysitting Dr. Garcia, who was a damn talented doctor.

Who was charming and had a good bedside manner.

Every single patient loved him. They would get giddy when he'd flash them a dimpled half smile. His eyes would twinkle, and even the toughest patients were won over.

It was so frustrating.

After working with Dr. Garcia all day, she had realized two things really quickly about him: he was an arrogant, cocky rival to her coveted fellowship, and he was *sexy* as hell. She had no real aversions to sexy as hell. She had no qualms about casual dating of men she was attracted to. She had learned that romantic entanglements, a future, or any of that nonsense was out of the question. Wanting those things had gotten her in trouble before. They were things she didn't need.

She didn't want.

Liar.

Adeline brushed off the thought and cursed at herself inwardly for letting it slip into her mind. Other surgeons, other medical professionals were off-limits. She'd learned that the hard way, and that painful lesson had almost cost her her career in medicine when she was just starting out.

Gregory had been her teacher and he'd been just as charming as Dr. Garcia.

Gregory had charmed her so well, she had no idea that he was married, and when she had broken it off, he had humiliated her. Thrown her under the bus.

She had had to change medical schools just to get her career back on track, and she had learned that relationships were a no-go zone. The only thing she needed in her life, the only thing she wanted right now, was that coveted position she'd been working *so hard* to get since she started as an intern at San Diego Mesa Hospital. After what Gregory had done, she had realized that to get what she wanted, she could only trust herself. No one else was going to have a hand in her future.

Heck, she'd been planning this since she was a student in medical school, when she had first heard of Dr. Maxine Wilder. An innovator in maternal-fetal medicine and obstetrics.

Dr. Wilder had saved so many lives.

Saved the hopeless cases.

And that's what Adeline wanted. She wanted to learn from the best. She wanted to save the hopeless cases. She wanted to prevent the pain of loss.

Her anger melted away as she thought of her mother. How it had been impossible for her mother to have another baby after Adeline, because of the rare genetic condition that plagued her family.

Thrombotic thrombocytopenic purpura. Also known as TTP. It caused blood clots and risked the life of the baby and the mother.

Her mom had developed it after Adeline was born. Although Mom had survived, the pregnancy that came after Adeline hadn't.

When her mother had been pregnant with Adeline, something had triggered this rare genetic disorder, causing it to kick in. A recessive gene that could lie dormant, but back then they hadn't known that. It was why Adeline had gone into medicine and loved it so much. Why she wanted to learn as much about TTP as she could.

And there was a part of her that blamed herself for causing her mom to be ill.

Her older brother hadn't triggered it.

It had been her.

A lump formed in her throat, and she had to take a deep breath to regain control of the emotions threatening to overtake her.

She wasn't going to let herself cry.

Crying got her nowhere. It just made her vulnerable, and that vulnerability could be used against her.

You cried and told me you loved me! Gregory had shouted. *Now you're ending this?*

You lied to me! You didn't tell me you were married. I asked you that when we started this relationship. It was a mistake. Adeline had wiped a tear from her eye.

He'd scowled at her. *If you report me, I'll ruin your career,* he'd threatened. *And I know you have high aspirations to help people like your mother.*

Adeline was cross she had thought of that. She hated the fact that she'd been thinking about Gregory today.

This wasn't about him.

It was about her career and working to make sure what happened to her mother didn't happen again.

That was Adeline's goal.

Medicine continued to advance, though, and Adeline had no doubt that now Dr. Wilder could have saved her other sibling.

And Adeline wanted to save more lives. The

most precious lives. In an attempt to make it up to her mother.

You could start by getting tested yourself like Mom wants.

Adeline sighed. She was terrified of getting tested, and since she wasn't interested in settling down and having a family or even a relationship, what was the point?

Pregnancy had triggered her mother's TTP and Adeline was never going to have a child.

No matter how much she secretly wanted one. She did want kids, but she was scared.

Scared that she had the gene and that people would find out; that she'd lose the baby; that she'd die or be too weak to continue her work.

So instead, she'd save lives. She would focus on this tough fellowship, which would completely test her mettle and give her a sense of purpose if she won the spot with Dr. Wilder. What she didn't need was an arrogant, good-looking, cocky new resident swaggering into her hospital and trying to take that spot from her.

It's not your hospital. Are you the chief?

Adeline laughed to herself.

She was being completely irrational. What she needed to do was have a nice glass of wine—a bottle was chilling in the fridge—and sit out on the beach for a bit. And forget all of this. Tomorrow was a new day. Sure, he was one more doctor, but she'd outlasted several and she could outlast Dr. Garcia too.

As she rounded the corner and headed down the street to the beach house she shared with a couple of other residents at the hospital, she saw a small rental van and boxes in the drive.

Today was the day they were getting a new roommate, as their previous roommate, Dennis, had accepted a position in Boston. She'd completely forgotten today was move-in day.

This day was just getting better and better.

Adeline was in no mood to make nice with her new roommate. She'd greet whoever this new roomie was, grab her bottle of wine and head out across the back patio to the beach and one of the deck chairs that was waiting for her. After today she was not in the mood.

Adeline sidestepped a few boxes and slipped through the open door.

"Sorry!" James shouted, coming down the stairs. "I can already tell by the look on your face you're fed up."

"Not with the boxes," Adeline grumbled, tossing her keys into large ceramic decorative clamshell by the door. "It's fine."

James cocked an eyebrow. "Clearly it's not."

"It was a tough day at work. I'm just going to open a bottle of wine and chill for a bit."

James made a face. "You were in such a good mood this morning. What happened?"

"New doctor. New competition. I don't want to talk about it. All I want is a drink."

James laughed. "Sure. Sherrie is already outside on the patio."

Adeline nodded and left James, who owned the beach house, to deal with their new roommate. She headed straight for the kitchen, grabbed her wine and a corkscrew, and headed out onto the back patio that backed straight into the white sand.

Sherrie was in one of the lounge chairs, a book on organ transplantation propped on her knees. Adeline didn't tend to have friends in her specialty, which is why she lived with Sherrie and James. They weren't in her specialty and she liked them well enough.

They weren't out for her job.

"What're you reading up on?" Adeline asked, plopping down next to her.

"Kidneys." Sherrie closed her book and sat up, eyeing the bottle. "You had a rough day?"

Adeline nodded, uncorking the bottle. "You know how we lost a bunch of residents, as they moved up to fellows and left the hospital for greener pastures? Just like Dennis did?"

Sherrie nodded. "Yes."

"One of the new residents is vying for *my* fellowship. Mine."

"Ugh."

"Exactly." Adeline sighed. "I wouldn't be so worried if I didn't think he was a threat."

"So he's good?" Sherrie asked.

"His recommendations were glowing. I heard Dr. Wilder talking about it. It's why she accepted him into her program." Adeline sighed again. "And he did a *decent* job when I was working with him today."

She didn't want to admit it, but Dr. Garcia was competent, which had her worried.

"Ugh," Sherrie said again, lying back and re-opening her book.

Adeline leaned back, too, still clutching her bottle of wine, staring up at the evening sky. "Want to get a bite to eat downtown?"

"I would, but I'm studying for this big surgery tomorrow. Dr. Thomas wants me to assist."

"No worries. Maybe I'll order in? I don't feel like cooking, especially with someone new moving in and their stuff everywhere."

Sherrie shut the book again and bolted upright. "Speaking of our new roommate, did you see him?"

"No. I haven't met him yet. I didn't even know he was a him until now."

"He's so gorgeous." Sherrie smiled dreamily. "I was seriously swooning when I saw him."

Adeline's stomach knotted. "Swooning?"

She had a bad feeling about this. The Fates wouldn't be that cruel, would they? She got up and went back into the house. James was a resident. They all were. He would have looked at SDMH for a new roommate.

James was a carrying a box up the stairs, a box that had the initials E.G.

No. No. No. Please no.

Her stomach dropped to the soles of her feet.

"What?" James asked. "You look distressed, like you've seen a ghost or something."

"Our new roommate…who is he?"

"You can ask him yourself. He's standing right behind you."

Dread crept down her spine, and Adeline turned around slowly.

"Dr. Turner, isn't it?" Dr. Elias Garcia asked, standing there with that same dimpled half smile he'd been sporting all day.

And there he was. Her competition. Looming there. He looked like a different man in his jeans and blue cotton shirt instead of the dark navy scrubs and white lab coat they wore at work. His sleeves were rolled up to his elbows, exposing his beautiful muscular forearms.

His dark eyes were twinkling, and his brown hair was a bit haphazard. His curls, usually a touch more tame at the hospital, were anything but. It suited him.

She was a bit breathless seeing him in this light. Not as the competition, but as a man she was completely and utterly attracted to.

Man, did she hate that.

He was as handsome as ever, and he was a temptation that Adeline didn't want. She didn't even want to think about it.

Remember what happened in medical school? Doctors are off-limits. He's your competition, your roommate. You don't casually date from SDMH. You don't. Remember that.

Though it was hard to think straight with him standing a few feet from her, smiling that charming smile he'd used on the patients today.

Well, she wasn't going to let it get to her.

No way.

Nothing was getting in her way this time.

Even if Elias made her weak in the knees.

Dammit.

Adeline suddenly hated Dennis for moving and taking that fellowship in Boston. She hated James for renting the attic room out to Dr. Garcia. How could he rent to him? First he was trying to take her fellowship with Dr. Wilder, and now he was living under the same roof.

She couldn't escape him.

"Are you okay, Dr. Turner?" Elias asked, his gaze tracking to the bottle of wine clenched in her fist.

"You're not moving in here," she stated fiercely, before sort of laughing because this whole thing was just absurd.

Elias looked confused. "I think I am."

Adeline laughed and shook her head. "No. No you're not."

"I am." And he took a step toward her, making her heart skip a beat. "Or are we going to have another discussion about who is the superior?"

Her cheeks heated. "You're not."

He grinned again, bending over to whisper in her ear. "I think you'll find I am."

"Well, hell!"

Well, hell?

Elias couldn't help but like Dr. Adeline Turner's fire. It made him chuckle inwardly. She certainly didn't hold her feelings back, which was a refreshing change and different from all the other women he knew and the foolish games they played. Games that might be fun during the chase, but thanks to his trust issues weren't as enjoyable after a while.

Adeline must be feeling the same way he was, seeing his rival standing in the hallway of his new home. And Dr. Adeline Turner was, without a doubt, his rival. He had known that from the moment he had met Adeline and seen the rapport she had with Dr. Wilder.

And she was talented.

He had learned that fast when he had worked with her today.

She was good.

Smart, quick on her feet and completely focused.

It would be a challenge to take her down, but Elias had never backed away from a challenge before.

It was obvious from her displeasure that she was not happy he was here.

Which meant that she saw him as a threat too. *Good.*

He was glad he was getting under her skin.

"Well, I'm glad we're off to a good start, roomie." He pushed past her and headed up the stairs, motioning for James to continue.

It was really too bad that Adeline was his competition, because if they weren't both vying for the same position, he would give her chase. She'd be fun to chase.

Blunt. To the point. Strong-willed and sexy as hell.

She hit all his buttons.

And he usually avoided women like that.

A woman like that was dangerous.

A woman like that could creep past his carefully constructed walls.

Walls that protected his heart.

He only ever wanted a nice quick fling these days, and Adeline Turner was dangerous. She was the kind of woman who would want more, she was serious. She didn't seem to be the kind of woman to have a fling. She was someone you had a relationship with. And he didn't want that. Elias was not interested in having a relationship. He had had a relationship before, one that he had given his whole heart to, and it had been torn to shreds. Elias was not going down that murky path again.

Quick flings.

A little bit of romance.

Some hot sex. That's all he wanted.

Adeline Turner had that same drive for career; he knew she wasn't interested in the fairy tale. Work was her passion, her spouse. You didn't have flings with women like that.

Just like it was for him, but he couldn't have a fiery fling with her. Not with the competition.

It could have been a hot, fun distraction.

He wasn't getting tied up in that. He was here to win a spot with Dr. Wilder, and he didn't trust or know Dr. Adeline Turner enough to get involved.

The last thing he needed was for her to turn Dr. Wilder against him.

Like the way Shea came between you and Aidan.

Elias sighed.

He didn't trust anyone but himself. Not even his family. He had trusted his brother once and look where that had gotten him.

Elias had learned his lesson.

"James," Adeline shouted as she followed him

up the stairs. "Are you serious? This is our new roommate?"

Elias rolled his eyes as James looked a bit pale. Elias took the box from James.

"Is she always so loud?" Elias asked, seeing if it rubbed Adeline the wrong way.

"Just a bit," James muttered under his breath.

"James!" Adeline snapped.

"I didn't know you two knew each other," James said. "Dr. Garcia is new in town and was looking for a place. We had a room. You know I rent to other employees at the hospital. I don't want any trouble, Adeline."

James pushed past Adeline, who was still fuming in the doorway. Elias couldn't help but smile at her there. She was kind of adorable, all infuriated.

Don't think of her like that.

Elias couldn't think about how cute she was. How he found her highly attractive.

He had to remember he was here for work.

Not romance.

He had to focus on his career rather than wondering how soft her blond hair was, with those beachy waves he loved. Full pink lips and curves in all the right places. Her dark eyes were bristling with annoyance.

He swore if she were a cartoon character, steam would be shooting out of her ears.

"Come on," Elias said jovially. "It can't be all that bad, can it?"

Those dark brown eyes of hers narrowed, and if he didn't know any better, he might think himself in trouble. It gave him a little zip of excitement.

Actually, he knew that he was in trouble.

"It's bad enough that you're going for a position I've worked hard for since day one of my internship, but now you're living above me?"

He grinned. "So I'm on top of you, then?"

Those peach-colored cheeks deepened with a blush. "You need to stay away from me."

It was a warning. Clear as day.

"That's kind of going to be hard since now we are both roommates and on Dr. Wilder's service." Elias knew he probably shouldn't push her, but something about him wanted to. He liked the fire that he could see bubbling beneath the surface.

She was strong.

It made his blood heat, the thrill of the chase taking over.

You can't think about her like that. She's not a conquest.

Adeline took a step back. "I know it'll be difficult but try your best. I am in it to obtain that position with Dr. Wilder. It is *my* position. We may be in close quarters and I can be professional, but that's it. Just stay out of my way."

Adeline turned on her heel and left in a huff.

Elias couldn't help but let his eyes wander over the way her jeans hugged her curves. The scrubs she'd worn at the hospital didn't do her any justice. They engulfed her, and the tight bun she wore didn't suit her at all.

It was like she was trying to hide herself under a bunch of layers.

Isn't that what you do too?

Didn't he feel safer with his white lab coat on? Especially when he was around his overbearing family. His family, who valued the family vineyard more than his academic successes. The coat was a visible reminder to them of what he had accomplished. Especially when he had to endure family functions with his brother, the man who had stolen his fiancée.

Aidan was his father's favorite. The son who had taken over the vineyard, settled down. Whereas Elias valued his career and education and had never settled down as had been expected of him. They had never understood that he didn't want a life working on the land, having his whole future dependent on whether the crop survived, whether there was enough rain or sun or anything. He hadn't wanted to break his back to earn a living. His father didn't understand Elias's need for learning and saw his life as easy, when there was nothing easy about medicine.

Every time Elias went home, he had to relive the pain over and over again. The reminder that he had grown apart from Shea, and Aidan had been there when he hadn't. That Aidan, once again, had had to take something from Elias the way he always did. Only, he couldn't take away Elias's career.

The white lab coat, the scrubs, his goal of saving the most vulnerable lives—that's what kept him safe.

That's what helped him to continue going.

It gave him courage to keep going.

It hardened his resolve.

Yeah, it would suck being under the same roof as his rival, especially one as tempting as Dr. Adeline Turner, but this was a competition, after all.

One he intended to win.

No matter what.

CHAPTER TWO

ADELINE WAS STILL in disbelief that her new room-mate was Elias. It figured that James would offer the room to him. It was as though the Fates were tormenting her.

How? the rational part of her asked, and she couldn't quite answer that.

All she knew was that she had to blame some-one, and James was a good scapegoat. Especially when she got up early the next day and made her way to the hospital. She wasn't a fan of early mornings on the best of days, so it was easy to be grumpy with James.

Yesterday her day had been bright and shiny, and within twenty-four hours it felt as though a cloud of doom and gloom were hovering over her.

Get to work and everything will be okay.

She wanted to arrive at SDMH before Elias got there. She just wanted to put him out of her mind and immerse herself in work.

On her walk there, she noodled out her anger somewhat and came to the conclusion that she might not be able to control the fact that Dr. Elias Garcia was living in the same house as her, but she could control her work.

She could control how she strived for excellence.

She did have the upper hand, because she had started her internship here. This was the place where she had progressed in her career and was known.

Dr. Wilder knew her and knew that she was an excellent surgeon.

Dr. Elias Garcia was new and he was charming. People were won over by his dazzling smile, but eventually they'd realize Adeline was dependable, reliable.

She was the one to beat and Dr. Garcia would fall to the side like all the others had.

Dr. Elias Garcia might have a bunch of accolades from his previous hospital and he might distract people by being the new thing, the new toy, but eventually they would rely on her. Like they always did.

Dr. Wilder had some adaptability, but in the end, Adeline knew that Dr. Wilder was a woman of routine and liked to keep things constant. And Adeline was her favorite, the person Dr. Wilder could trust with her practice. She just had to keep reminding herself of that.

Adeline smiled to herself as she walked in through the front doors of the hospital. The sun was shining, it wasn't too hot and it wasn't cold. She was here before anyone else in her program and she was going to get started on preparing Dr. Wilder's charts after she grabbed herself a coffee from the coffee cart.

It could be the perfect day. And maybe today she could work on consultations. She'd shown Elias around. He said he was a big deal, so he could handle his second day on his own.

Adeline was going to avoid Elias as much as humanly possible.

"Good morning, Dr. Turner," a smooth, deep voice said from behind her.

A shiver of dread coursed down her spine. She slowly turned around to see Dr. Elias Garcia standing a few feet behind her.

He was already in his navy scrubs and white lab coat. In one hand he had a cup of coffee from the cart, and in the other he carried a tablet.

He looked as good as he had last night. Actually, it looked as if he had never even left the hospital. Which was crazy. She knew he had. She'd heard him moving stuff around all night.

"You look tired," he said offhandedly.

"Well, someone was loud and inconsiderate all night."

"Not all night." He grinned. "Although I've been known to go all night."

Adeline rolled her eyes. "Sure."

"Well, you must've been hearing things or were dreaming about me."

She clenched her fists and took a deep breath. As much as he was driving her crazy, he was sexy, and something about him just drew her in.

She hated that smile.

No, you don't.

She liked it. It made her blood heat, and it infuriated her that she had no control over her physical reaction.

Adeline prided herself on her control.

She needed to regain it.

Right now.

Focus, Adeline. He's the enemy.

"Are those Dr. Wilder's charts?" she asked, eyeing the tablet with dread.

Elias looked down at the tablet. "Ah, yes. I thought since I was here, I would get started on organizing Dr. Wilder's charts and check up on a patient who was admitted last night."

"There was a patient admitted last night?" Adeline asked, shocked as she pulled out her phone to see if she had been paged. She had not.

"Well, after I got all my things moved in. I had a quick shower and I decided to head to the hospital, because I forgot something and there was a woman in the ER. She was presenting with what appeared to be a blood pressure problem and Dr. Wilder was there. She asked me to assist. We stabilized the patient. I spent the night watching her at Dr. Wilder's request."

It felt like Adeline's world was crumbling down around her. Usually she was the one who was called when a case came in overnight.

It's why she lived so close to the hospital.

It should have been me. The thought replayed in her head over and over again, and she could almost hear her mother's voice telling her not to be selfish. There were worse things in the world, and she should just be grateful for being alive.

And she was, but this was her fellowship.

She wasn't going to let anyone take it from her.

She wasn't going to let another man ruin her chance.

He's not Gregory.

And she hated that once again she was thinking of him.

That Elias made her think of the biggest mistake of her life.

Adeline forced a smile on her face. "Well, maybe you should go home and get some rest if you've been here all night? I can take care of the charts." She reached out to take the tablet, but he pulled back.

Elias's eyes narrowed and he smiled, but this wasn't the warm, charming smile that he usually flashed in the direction of his patients. The smile that made their patients swoon.

Adeline knew this kind of smile.

She knew the determination behind it.

This smile said, *Bring it on.*

"I thank you for your concern about my well-being, Dr. Turner, but I'm quite all right to take care of the charts this morning."

Adeline was going to argue further when she saw Dr. Wilder walking across the lobby toward them.

She snapped her mouth shut.

"Ah, Dr. Turner, I'm glad you're here. Has Dr. Garcia filled you in on our patient?" Dr. Wilder asked brusquely.

"Briefly, but he hasn't fully gone over the chart with me."

Elias shot her a side-eye, and she couldn't help but smile at him with just a bit of smugness.

Dr. Wilder was completely oblivious to this interaction. "Good. Good. Well, Dr. Garcia was a lifesaver to me last night with this particular patient, but it is most likely we will have to deliver the baby early. Dr. Garcia was top of his class for neonatology and pediatrics, and Dr. Turner, you are my right-hand woman when it comes to obstetrical surgery. You're both talented surgeons. I want you to work together on this case. We need to keep the fetus *in utero* for as long as possible, and we need to figure out what's happening with the patient. Is it preeclampsia, a thyroid or cardiac issue? There are a lot of 'could bes,' and I need the answers."

"You want us to work together?" Adeline asked, slightly choking on the lump that had formed in her throat. Somehow, this day wasn't going well either.

This was something she had been waiting for. A chance to fly solo on a case. To prove herself to Dr. Wilder.

The only thing she hadn't counted on was working with Dr. Garcia.

But if her chance came from taking the devil by the hand and selling her soul, the devil being Dr. Garcia, she was going to accept it with open arms.

Even if she got burned.

"Dr. Wilder, will you not be handling this?" Dr. Garcia asked, obviously just as shocked.

Dr. Wilder smiled, looking back and forth between them. "You two are the best residents, both vying for a fellowship in one of the toughest practices of medicine. I like to teach in the Socratic method as often as I can. It was how I was taught. I will be available for consult, but this case, this patient and the life of her child are in your hands."

Dr. Wilder didn't say anything else.

"Thank you," Adeline said, taking the tablet from Elias as he processed the information. It was a good thing he was just as shocked as she was. "The patient is in good hands, Dr. Wilder."

Elias cleared his throat. "Yes. Thank you, Dr. Wilder."

Dr. Wilder nodded. "Good. I look forward to hearing your thoughts. The patient's labs should be ready. I'd start there."

Without saying anything else, she walked away.

Elias stood in front of Adeline. His arms were crossed, and he was clutching his paper coffee cup so tightly, Adeline was a bit worried it would be crushed, and the coffee would go everywhere.

"So. We have to work together on my patient," he stated stiffly.

"Our patient now," Adeline corrected him.

"Fine. Our patient." He finished his drink, tossed the deformed coffee cup into a garbage can and took a step closer to her. "Look, I know we're in a competition, but I'm sure that you can't let this bleed into your work with the patient."

"I am professional if that's what you're asking. Are you?"

"I am," he said, his voice dropping as he came even closer. "Very professional."

The way he said *very* made her blood heat. Like there was a promise in that. And if it had been any other man she was attracted to, in another profession, it would be a promise she'd certainly like to experience.

"Good," she said, finding her voice and hoping it wasn't shaking. "Shall we go see our patient?"

A lazy smile spread on his face as he looked her up and down.

"Shouldn't you change into your scrubs first?" He was standing so close to her, his breath was hot and fanned her neck, causing a sliver of heat to course through her veins. It was in that microsecond when her body reacted to him being so close that he slipped the tablet out of her hands. She couldn't help but cede it to him on that smart play.

Damn him.

"Fine. You're right. Shall we meet at the lab? You can retrieve the results and then we'll have a consultation before we see the patient?"

He nodded. "That sounds good, Dr. Turner."

Adeline walked away from him. She needed to get her head in the game and not let Elias or her attraction to him manipulate her further.

Sure, she was working with the enemy, but this could be used to her advantage too.

And that made her feel a lot better about her chances and her place in Dr. Wilder's fellowship.

Elias didn't have to wait long at the lab for Adeline to show up. Gone were the flattering street clothes that accentuated her curves. She was buried under scrubs that were slightly too big for her. It was her armor and he respected that. He understood that.

His scrubs were his armor too.

Elias wished that he didn't have to work with Adeline, but her focus was more on obstetrics, and his focus was more on the welfare of the fetus.

Judging from his tests last night, the fetus was stable.

Even if he didn't want to admit it, he needed Adeline on this case. The thought of needing her threw him, because he had learned to rely on himself a long time ago.

He would work with Adeline, but he had to make sure it was professional.

Nothing else.

It irritated him that he needed her knowledge.

Though he didn't want to admit it, she was smart, and he could use her help.

He was so frustrated with himself.

This was not what he had planned when he took this placement.

Of course, he hadn't planned on meeting someone like Adeline either.

"Do you have the results?" she asked.

"I do. Shall we head into a consult room and talk about it?" Elias had a feeling any talk with Adeline could be charged and heated, if past behavior was any indication of future behavior.

"Sure."

Elias found an empty consult room and held the door open for her. Once she took a seat at the table, he shut the door and sat across from her.

"Tell me about the patient," Adeline said, getting right down to business.

"Mrs. Bryant is a thirty-four-year-old gravida three para two patient who presented last night with a BP of one-thirty-three over ninety and tachycardia. Also, some indigestion."

"Tachycardia? Indigestion?"

"We did an ECG. Whatever it was, the heart rate returned to normal. We did a swab of her nose. No COVID or SARS."

Something was nagging at the back his mind, something that seemed familiar to him. It had been bothering him since Mrs. Bryant was admitted and he hated the fact that he couldn't figure it out. Then again, he was just starting out his obstetrics rotation. At least he was starting with the best. Adeline was a good OB-GYN attending—he had looked her up to know who he had to watch out for. Hopefully she could come up with an answer. He could tell that Adeline was mulling it over too.

"Did the patient have protein in her urine?"

Elias opened the lab results. "No, but her peripheral smear shows schistocytes."

Adeline's eyes widened. "Schistocytes, you say?"

"Yes. Why?"

He knew schistocytes were red blood cells that were jagged, irregular and only present in certain diseases.

"Was an ADAMTS13 level drawn?" There was something in her voice, a tremble, just a momentary lapse. ADAMTS13 was an enzyme involved with a large protein important in blood clotting. An elevated level could mean that Mrs. Bryant had a blood clotting issue.

"No, but we can have that done given her peripheral smear."

Adeline nodded, but it still seemed like she was in a bit of a trance.

"Let's go see the patient." Adeline stood up. "I'd like to examine her."

"Okay. We can get the draw done for the ADAMTS13 level too." Elias stood. "What're you thinking?"

Adeline sighed. "Thrombotic thrombocytopenic purpura. TTP. I think Mrs. Bryant's issue is a blood clotting issue. Which could put both her and the baby at risk."

Elias was annoyed he hadn't thought of that. But he dealt with babies after they were delivered prematurely from TTP. He didn't deal with the mothers, but it made sense. "Of course."

He'd seen cases of it, though it was rare and nobody knew why it happened in pregnancy, but if they didn't get a handle on it, it was almost always fatal left untreated.

"Have you seen TTP before?" Adeline asked as they left the consult room. Elias mouthed and counted on his fingers. Adeline seemed momentarily surprised by his idiosyncrasy.

"A couple of times, not from diagnosis, but

in the operating room when we were delivering the fetus early, and then I worked with the pediatric and neonatal team to save the preemie's life. Have you?"

"I've lived it," Adeline muttered, and then she cursed under her breath as she pushed the up button on the elevator. "Forget I said that."

"Can't really. I have an eidetic memory."

She cocked an eyebrow. "Really? That's fascinating."

"I think so." They shared an awkward smile, waiting for the elevator. "So, about this living through it thing?"

"My mother developed TTP after my birth. I was a premature baby, born at thirty-two weeks. My mother had the even rarer form of TTP, the genetic version. The gene can lie dormant, and pregnancy could be one of the things that triggers the dormant gene to wake up. Usually, it's just a rare complication of pregnancy and it goes away after. Other times, it sticks around."

"I'm sorry," Elias whispered. "So, has she had a flare-up recently?"

"No. Thankfully. She's been begging me to get genetic testing, but…" Adeline pushed the button a couple more times. "I don't even know why I'm telling you this."

"It's okay. Honestly, sometimes I work with preemies and I think of my nephew who was premature. I was fifteen when he was born. I was uncle to this tiny, fragile human who might not live, and I knew what I wanted to do. And I was a preemie. It was my destiny, I suppose."

Adeline's expression softened and his heart beat a bit faster. "It was the same for me. I wanted to save the sibling I lost. Help other women not feel that pain my mother did."

Elias nodded. "And so you shall."

He didn't know why he said that. It just slipped out.

She had told him something personal and he had offered her that comfort. Like a close friend might, though they were anything but friends, and he hoped he hadn't offended her or said something out of line.

Adeline smiled at him shyly, and his heart skipped a beat. Pink tinged her cheeks as an awkward silence fell between them.

The elevator door dinged and opened. Someone got off and they got in. The doors slid shut.

"I'd appreciate it if you kept this to yourself. I don't like my business spread all over the hospital," she said, breaking the silence.

"Okay, but you should get your genetic testing done."

"Why?" she asked.

"Well, if you decided to have a family one day..."

The shy smile instantly disappeared. Her pink lips pursed together in a straight line.

"I don't think that's your business. We don't know each other," she snapped.

"I'm sorry if I overstepped some boundary. I didn't mean to. I just thought seeing as you're a doctor, you'd want it done."

"I don't ever plan on having a family, so that won't happen, Dr. Garcia."

Her answer disappointed him, and he didn't know why. It wasn't as though he ever wanted a family. He didn't want to settle down, but there was something about Adeline's finality that bothered him. Like his shot with her had melted away. Even though all he cared about was his career, which involved no family ties.

Liar. You want those things. You're just too afraid.

Family was complicated. He hadn't gotten along with his father since he had turned away from running the vineyard and decided on medicine. No matter what Elias did, he couldn't please his father.

Ever.

His younger brother was always better.

Even a better husband.

Don't think of Shea.

The elevator stopped on their floor and Adeline got off, with him following her. He shouldn't have pestered Adeline. He shouldn't have pried.

Adeline's personal life was not his concern. He couldn't get involved.

She was stubborn, he'd give her that. He admired that about her.

And the more he admired her, the more he wanted her.

Even though that was not possible.

CHAPTER THREE

ADELINE'S PULSE WAS thundering in her ears.

She hated it when TTP presented. Thankfully, there was only one other time it had when she'd been on rotation in the ER.

It had been that diagnosis which caught the attention of Dr. Wilder, but it had been that diagnosis which terrified her to her very core and reminded her of all the things she could have.

She wanted to help save those afflicted by it, but it scared her too. It took every ounce of strength to gain a hold of her emotions.

Maybe it's not TTP?

Only she shook that optimistic little voice away.

She was never wrong about TTP. She'd seen it so much growing up.

Your mom is okay, kids.

Her dad had looked tired. There'd been dark circles under his eyes.

This won't happen again. Not like this.

Adeline had been scared as she and her brother

were ushered into their mother's hospital room. Her mother had lain there, pale, weak and broken.

The kids are here, Bev.

Okay...

Her mother had just whispered, not looking at them and not sounding like herself. Just a fragment, a ghost.

Adeline shook that thought away as they approached the patient's room. Mrs. Bryant had a jaundiced tinge to her skin. Adeline could see it even from the door, and her stomach knotted knowing it was TTP from that first glance. She resolved right then and there she would save her patient.

"Mrs. Bryant, I'm Dr. Garcia. We met when you were admitted, remember?"

"Yes, Dr. Garcia. I remember," Mrs. Bryant said quietly, smiling.

"This is Dr. Turner. She's an obstetrics fellow working with Dr. Wilder on her service."

Mrs. Bryant smiled at Adeline, and Adeline could see the exhaustion, the worry in the patient's eyes.

"How are you feeling, Mrs. Bryant?" Adeline asked gently as she pulled out her stethoscope to listen to the baby's heartbeat.

"A headache, some indigestion...again."

"A headache? When did that start?" Adeline asked the nurse.

"About an hour ago," the nurse said. "Her BP was normal, though."

Adeline nodded and listened to the heartbeat of the baby, which was strong. She stopped listening and palpated Mrs. Bryant's abdomen, and everything felt normal.

"We're going to do another blood draw. We need to rule out some things and I'd like to do an ultrasound and check on the baby if that's okay, Mrs. Bryant?" Adeline asked.

Mrs. Bryant nodded. "Of course."

"I can do the ultrasound now," Elias said.

Adeline then checked the patient's skin. She was looking for the purpura, the small bruises under the skin that would confirm the thrombi in the small blood vessels.

She saw them on the underside of Mrs. Bryant's arm and then on the belly where she had palpated.

Elias did the ultrasound, so Mrs. Bryant was distracted, watching her baby. Adeline leaned over to watch.

"Baby looks good," Elias said. "Strong heartbeat. Good amount of amniotic fluid. The baby is stable."

Adeline nodded and turned back to the nurse.

"I need an ADAMTS13 draw. Put a rush on it. I need you to also start a dose of betamethasone."

"Yes, Dr. Turner," the nurse said.

Adeline turned to the patient. "Mrs. Bryant,

your baby is strong, but on the off chance your blood pressure goes up or the baby goes into distress, we'll start a medication to help with lung maturity. That's the betamethasone I just ordered."

"Okay," Mrs. Bryant said, her voice shaking.

Adeline smiled at Mrs. Bryant and squeezed her shoulder gently. "It'll be okay. This is standard. You're in good hands."

"I will continue to monitor your baby," Elias reassured the patient. "The baby is fine."

"Thank you, Doctors." Mrs. Bryant closed her eyes. "It's a lot to process."

"It is, but you're stable and we're going to watch you." Adeline and Elias left the patient's room and walked down the hall to the nurses' station.

"What're you thinking?" Elias asked. "You're awfully quiet."

"And how do you know that? You only met me yesterday."

"You were a lot more vocal and engaged yesterday. Very opinionated, especially with regard to my moving in," he teased.

Adeline sighed, but couldn't help but relax just a bit.

"Fine. I'm troubled. Mrs. Bryant has purpura."

Elias frowned. "And with the headache and indigestion?"

"It's TTP. Whether it's genetic or acquired, I

won't know until genetic testing is done, but we have to keep her admitted and monitor both her and the baby."

"We can't go to Dr. Wilder with a hunch," Elias stated.

"I'm usually not wrong. The ADAMTS13 test will determine it. The nurse is giving the patient betamethasone now. If it is TTP, we need to consult with hematology and start TPE to thin her blood and to help with clots."

Elias nodded. "We'll see what the blood work says. We'll keep a close eye on the baby."

Adeline's phone vibrated in her pocket. She pulled it out. "Dr. Wilder needs me in OR three. An emergency surgery."

"I got the same page." Elias flashed his phone. "The baby must be in distress."

"Let's go, then."

"You lead the way. I'm still learning this place."

Adeline smiled. "Come on."

Adeline had to get her mind off the TTP. She had to compartmentalize it away, like she always did because she was a professional.

Right now, there was another life to save.

Adeline focused on her patients, working in tandem with Dr. Wilder as they performed an open fetal surgery on the baby. By half delivering it, but not cutting the cord, they could perform surgery on the spina bifida.

Dr. Wilder had been planning to do a feto-scopic surgery, using small incisions and passing instruments through to operate on the baby *in utero*, but there was a complication and they had to open up the mother instead.

The baby was thirty weeks along, but the mother had blood pressure problems and Dr. Wilder had called in the neonatology team on the off chance the baby would have to be delivered fully.

"How is the mother doing?" Dr. Wilder asked.

"Her blood pressure is rising," the anesthesiologist said.

Dr. Wilder's brown furrowed. "Preeclampsia."

"So we may have to deliver?" Adeline asked as she gently worked on the tiny life still attached to her mother.

Dr. Wilder nodded. "If the BP continues to rise we'll have no choice. Dr. Garcia, can you come here?"

Elias stepped forward, gowned and ready. "Yes, Dr. Wilder?"

"You've performed a spina bifida repair on an infant, yes?" Dr. Wilder asked.

"Yes. I have."

"Then take my place. I may have to deliver and close the mother."

"Of course, Dr. Wilder."

Adeline watched as Elias took the spot at the

table across from her. His large hands moved delicately as he assisted her without guidance.

He knew what to do. Just like she did.

Don't be so shocked. He was an attending too, after all.

"Hmm. Just what I thought," Dr. Wilder remarked, watching them.

"Dr. Wilder?" Adeline asked.

"You two. You work well together. In tandem. I thought so." Dr. Wilder moved to attend to the mother.

Adeline shook her head and went back to work.

"You disagree?" Elias asked quietly.

"This is our first surgery together. Hardly enough to base a whole opinion on," Adeline muttered.

"Oh, I think it's enough," Elias said. "Some surgeons instinctively fit together. They know what to do and can intuitively predict the next step of the other surgeon. I think we move and work well together."

Heat crept up her neck, and she was glad of the surgical mask and gear hiding her blush because of what he was insinuating. How they intuitively knew how to move together, again with that promise of something more.

You can't go there.

She had to remind herself of that. Elias was getting too close for her liking. He was getting in her head.

Especially after he had suggested she should get the genetic testing because she wanted a family.

His presumption had been too personal, and it had made her uncomfortable.

She was frustrated that she still hadn't done it, but she was too afraid about what it would say.

You're afraid it'll be positive, and you'll never have a child.

An alarm went off.

"She's crashing!" someone shouted.

"Turner, I need you here!" Dr. Wilder shouted. "Garcia, we're delivering the baby. Ready the team to take the baby to the NICU."

Adeline dropped her instruments and made her way to the mother.

The NICU team came and helped Dr. Garcia finish up.

"Cutting the cord," Dr. Wilder announced as Adeline clamped it.

They delivered the baby, and Adeline watched from the corner of her eye as Elias gently scooped up the tiny infant, stepping in to save the baby's life while she saved the mother's. He might seem like an arrogant brute to her, but watching him handle that tiny baby, so small in his strong hands, made her melt just a bit.

"When the baby is stable, Garcia, I need you here," Dr. Wilder shouted. "She's bleeding out and I need all hands. Hang some more blood."

Adeline turned back to the work. The patient's blood pressure was dangerously high, and Adeline drowned everything out to focus on the task at hand. She didn't even notice Elias had returned until she heard him speaking beside her.

"The baby is stable and in the NICU," he said.

After that, time stood still as she and Elias worked side by side with Dr. Wilder to save a life.

Dr. Wilder was right. Elias was right. They worked well together. Seamlessly.

He might be her competition, but they were a dream surgical team.

Even though she hated admitting it.

It was easy to work with Dr. Elias Garcia.

Elias now really knew what that old saying of "out of the frying pan and into the fire" meant. He was exhausted as they had spent hours repairing vessels and the uterus of the mother. Not to mention having done the spina bifida repair on the baby before that.

He was used to long surgeries, but not two surgeries in a row. In Houston his focus had always been on the baby, not the mother.

So he was drained, but that was why he was here.

To learn.

Still, he was beat.

All he could do was sit on the bench outside

the operating room, trying to stretch out the knot in his back.

Adeline came out of the scrub room and sat down next to him.

Yesterday she would have shouted something ridiculous like *This is my bench. Get lost!* But it seemed she'd finally accepted him.

For now.

"That was grueling! I thought some pediatric surgeries were hard," Elias admitted. "But two lives on the line?"

"Right?" Adeline sighed. "You did well. I guess my gut was right to be worried about you."

There was a twinkle in her eyes as she said it, and he couldn't help but smile back at her. There was so much he liked about her. She was smart, determined, talented and beautiful.

Stop finding reasons to like her.

She wouldn't care two figs about him if she got the position.

She'd swoop in and take what was his. Just like Aidan had done.

Elias had to remind himself she was the enemy. He would work with her, but he was at San Diego Mesa Hospital to win.

"Dr. Wilder wants a meeting first thing tomorrow about Mrs. Bryant. She has other residents on call tonight. She told us to go home and rest."

Elias nodded. "I won't argue. Shall we walk

home together, or do you own the sidewalk too?"
he teased.

She slugged his arm playfully. "I suppose we
could walk home together. Meet you out front in
twenty minutes?"

Elias nodded as she stood. "Sounds good."

Adeline started to walk away, but then turned
back, her arms crossed. Elias braced himself for
the worst, but instead she smiled at him.

Softly.

"Good job today, Dr. Garcia." A pink blush
tinged her cheeks, and she turned quickly and
left.

His pulse quickened at the compliment.

"Same," he whispered.

He got up and made his way to the NICU before he went to change.

The NICU always calmed him. He had started
out here, and his fifteen-year-old nephew Manny
had spent his first days here too.

He saw the little girl they had saved, and she
was thriving. Her father, in a gown, stood by the
incubator.

Elias smiled. There was a time in his life when
he would have given almost anything to be a father, when he'd thought he'd marry Shea after he
got through with all his training, but then that had
fallen through.

So fatherhood was not in the cards for him.

He couldn't even remember the last time he'd

been home to Napa and the family vineyard. It had been two years. He couldn't recall the actual visit. Only that it had been brief.

He felt his family's disappointment in him that he hadn't taken over the vineyard. His brother was married to the woman he had loved, and they were now running the land.

They rubbed it in his face every time he came home. They let him know he was the inadequate son, an inadequate choice for a husband.

A disappointment. He saw the disappointment in his father's face.

It's why he hadn't been home for so long. He was tired of feeling inadequate.

Elias's heart sank and he walked away. There was no use brooding over broken, buried dreams or giving a second thought to the family he'd lost.

CHAPTER FOUR

WHY AM I waiting here?

Adeline was regretting agreeing to walk home with Elias when he asked her.

She should have said no, but how could she say no to her new roommate?

She might not want to get close to him, but she didn't want to be a jerk either.

And now she had been waiting for over twenty minutes.

Adeline was worried that Elias had left without her, that he was tricking her and she was being played for a fool.

He's not Gregory.

Only she couldn't shake that thought from her head.

She'd been burned once, and she wouldn't be burned again.

She was two seconds from leaving when she saw Elias heading across the lobby toward her. He looked completely different out of his scrubs and in his street clothes, but both ways he looked absolutely delicious.

It made her feel hot and bothered and irritated that she was letting those thoughts in.

Again.

You can't have him.

She couldn't get involved with someone she worked with, someone she was competing with.

She couldn't be pushed out of this program.

"Sorry, I wanted to check on the baby we delivered, so I went up to the NICU," he said, a bit out of breath as if he had been rushing. He looked her up and down and that slow perusal made her stomach do backflips in anticipation, although she wasn't anticipating anything with him because nothing was going to happen.

"You look nice."

"I'm wearing the same thing I was wearing this morning," she stated.

"Except you're wearing your hair down." He reached out and touched it. "I like seeing it down."

"I pull it back because we're in and out of the operating room or delivery room most days." She nervously tucked back her hair behind her ear and cleared her throat. Not liking the way her body reacted to his touch.

"How is the baby doing?"

"Good." But there was something he was holding back, and it set off her alarm bells. Something was bothering him, and Adeline had an inkling it wasn't about the baby. But it wasn't her problem and it wasn't her business.

It was bad enough she had let personal information slip, that she had let her guard down.

She didn't like the way he was affecting her.

They walked silently side by side.

It was a beautiful San Diego summer evening. Breezy, but warm. The patios and restaurants were starting to get busy, but it was not yet the dinner rush. This was one of her favorite times of day. It was her favorite kind of evening in San Diego.

"Are you from San Diego?" she asked, trying to make conversation.

"No. Napa."

"I'm from San Francisco. My parents still live there."

"So we're both Californians by birth. Something else we have in common, besides the preemie thing." He smiled quickly, but then looked away, making Adeline uncomfortable with the silent tension between them.

"Where did you go to school? Where did you do your internship?" she asked, trying to break the awkwardness she felt. It made her think of Elias and the way she reacted to him. The way he was getting under her skin.

"What's with the twenty questions?" he asked, teasing.

"Trying to get to know my competition,"

she teased right back, but instantly that tension slipped away.

Elias laughed. "You're quite funny and your smile is lovely. Usually you're so dour. Especially when you're looking at me."

Adeline rolled her eyes. "I take my job very seriously."

"It doesn't hurt to smile."

"That lets people in, and I made that mistake once early in my career. It won't happen again." And she was annoyed that she had let something slip once more.

What is wrong with me?

What was it about Elias that made her open up?

Adeline pulled out her keys as they headed to the front door of the beach house they shared. She knew Sherrie was still in a transplant surgery and James was on night rotation in the emergency room. It was just the two of them at home tonight.

Think of something else.

She opened the door. "Well, I'll have a quick bite and a glass of wine on the patio. Today was intense."

"Can I join you?" he asked.

Say no. Say no.

"Sure."

"How about I order some Thai food?"

"That sounds great."

"You grab the wine and head outside. I'll wait

for the food," Elias offered. "You can pay me back later."

"Oh? What with, a fellowship?" she teased.

Elias laughed and winked. Adeline headed into the kitchen and pulled out the bottle of wine she had opened yesterday but hadn't drunk. She grabbed two wineglasses, kicked off her shoes and headed out onto the back patio.

The sun was just starting to set, casting an orange glow over the white sand, and the breeze blowing in off the Pacific was heaven.

Calming.

It had always calmed her to sit by the water in San Francisco. If she closed her eyes, she could almost see herself there, back among the tall trees, and feel the whisper of fog rolling in off the bay.

As she closed her eyes, though, those calming thoughts melted away to the sight of the purpura under Mrs. Bryant's skin. She was still worried about her patient.

"It'll be here in twenty minutes," Elias said, but then paused. "What's wrong?"

"I was thinking of Mrs. Bryant. Going over our presentation to Dr. Wilder."

"The TTP diagnosis?" he asked.

Adeline nodded and poured him a glass of wine. "It's just always so hard to watch. Maybe I should go back?"

"She's stable. She's fine," Elias said. "There's nothing more you can do."

He was right, but there was a part of her that felt she couldn't trust him. That maybe he would swoop in while her back was turned and take credit for their work.

Elias isn't Gregory.

Only, how could she be certain of that? She didn't know him.

The doorbell rang and Elias got up. "Food's here. I'll be back. You set the table and we'll eat out here."

"Sounds good." Adeline got up and went into the kitchen, grabbing dishes from the cupboards and taking them out to the small patio table. Elias brought out the food.

The pad thai smelled amazing.

You need to walk away.

She had to put some distance between her and Elias. She wouldn't let what happened between her and Gregory happen again.

She'd been a fool to fall in love with Gregory.

This was why she refused to date anyone in her workplace.

Who said anything about dating?

This was just a friendly dinner, nothing more.

She could have dinner with her colleague, with her roommate, because that's all this was.

They sat down to eat as the sun set and the solar lights came on, creating a soft glow.

"Full moon tonight. James will be busy in the ER," she remarked, trying to make small talk.

"Why is that, you think?" Elias asked.

"I don't know. Of course, full moons also see a lot of babies being born. I'm glad I'm off duty tonight."

"I think a lot of babies are conceived during a full moon too." His voice was husky and there was a twinkle in his eyes. A twinkle that was dangerous.

Her heart skipped a beat, and it was suddenly very hard to swallow. Her food tasted like sawdust in her mouth.

"So, tell me about this vineyard you grew up on," she said, trying to change the subject. To get her mind off her attraction.

Elias looked confused. "Did I tell you that?"

"No, but I figured it out."

"How?" he asked, amazed.

She grinned. "You grew up in Napa and you grimace, ever so slightly, when you take a sip of wine. So you know something about quality."

Elias chuckled. "Fine. I did. My family has been making wine for a century. The vineyard has been passed down from father to son since the beginning."

"So, are you going to leave medicine for the vineyard one day?"

His brow furrowed. "No. No, I have a more

perfect younger brother who stepped up where I failed."

She knew she had hit a hot button there, and she couldn't help but wonder what family would be disappointed by having a surgeon for a son.

"Well, your family is crazy," she said. "Having a talented physician as a son is something to be proud of."

A strange look crossed his face, one that made her feel hot all over.

"You're quite beautiful, you know," he said.

"Don't," she whispered.

"What?"

"Don't compliment me."

Elias leaned back in his chair. "Why?"

"We're rivals." She got up to clean the table. He stood and touched her arm, causing a jolt of electricity to course through her, her body reacting to his touch.

"Rivals can still compliment one another."

She cocked an eyebrow. "Can they?"

"When it's deserved," he said softly. "And from what I've seen the last couple of days…you're fierce competition."

Her pulsed raced at his compliment. That smile, the twinkle in his eyes. She understood how he won people over.

There was something about him. She was attracted to him and maybe, just maybe, if she kissed him, she would stop being so flustered around him.

That's absurd.

Still, the more she thought about it, the more she couldn't stop thinking about it.

And though it went against everything she kept telling herself over and over again, she couldn't fight it anymore.

She wanted Elias Garcia. She had wanted him the moment she first saw him. And perhaps if she gave in to that hunger, the driving need that had burned in her blood since they had met, she could get on with her life. She could get him out of her system. He took a step closer to her, as if he were thinking the same thing, as if he were fighting the same thing she was feeling too.

The attraction.

"Elias," she whispered, her heart racing. She needed to step away from him. This was too dangerous.

"I want to kiss you, Adeline. No, scratch that. I'm going to kiss you, Adeline."

Adeline nodded and met him halfway. She was more than willing enough to get swept away in this moment.

Elias's hands were in her hair as he kissed her, passionate and intense. Just the way she wanted.

Just the way she needed.

All she wanted was the heat, the pleasure and the rush with him.

No. You can't do this.

She pushed him away as the kiss ended. "I can't."

Even though she wanted to.

"Sorry, Adeline. I couldn't resist."

Adeline found it hard to breathe. "Nothing to be sorry about, but I think I'm going to bed. Thank you for dinner. I owe you one."

Elias nodded and looked away. "Night, Adeline."

"Night." She moved quickly, putting distance between her and Elias before she did something she regretted.

Before she made the same mistake twice.

Elias had tossed and turned all night thinking about that kiss. He didn't know what had come over him. Adeline was off-limits, but that kiss… he couldn't get that kiss out of his head.

It fired his blood.

If she had been any other woman, he knew that kiss would have led to more, but he was glad Adeline had put a stop to it.

If she hadn't, he would have.

Would you?

He scrubbed his hand over his face and poured himself some bad coffee from the doctors' lounge. He had to get his head straight. They had the presentation about Mrs. Bryant for Dr. Wilder today.

He wasn't going to blow it.

Adeline walked into the doctors' lounge. His heart skipped a beat when he saw her. She paused awkwardly, hovering in the doorway.

Her cheeks tinged pink.

"Good morning," she said, clearing her throat.

"Morning." He took a sip of his coffee.

"How's the coffee?" she asked, not looking at him.

"Terrible." He smiled and set it down.

"Look, about last night…" Adeline trailed off.

"It's fine," he said, trying to reassure her.

"Is it?" she asked, as if she didn't believe him.

"It is. It was a mistake. It won't happen again. Trust me."

A strange look passed across her face. "Okay." Adeline poured herself a cup.

"You ready for this presentation?" he asked.

"I'm always ready." She looked at him, but gone was the shy, uncertain look he had briefly seen before. Back was the same determined surgeon he had met a couple of days ago. The surgeon he thought was sexy as hell.

Get that thought out of your head.

It was bad enough that he had kissed her, but he couldn't let his thoughts derail his chance at this job, and it was obvious by the way Adeline had snapped back that she wasn't going to let them get in her way either.

"Well, let's go," Adeline said. "Unless you need another cup of coffee?"

"I'm fine." He finished the remnants of the awful, bitter coffee and tossed the cup in the garbage.

He followed her out into the hall and fell into step beside her. All they had to do was present their findings about Mrs. Bryant to Dr. Wilder, and Elias hoped that they wouldn't have to work so closely together again.

Dr. Wilder thinks you and Adeline work well together.

And that thought troubled him, because he had the sinking suspicion that he was going to be stuck working alongside Adeline until Dr. Wilder made her decision about who got the fellowship.

He would be stuck working within arms' length of his temptation.

Which was a dangerous thing.

They found Dr. Wilder waiting for them, pacing around a conference room. She turned on her heel and looked at them both.

"Well, Doctors? What's the diagnosis?"

"TTP," Adeline said. "The patient's blood draws confirmed it and so did the presence of purpura."

Dr. Wilder didn't say anything. Her cold, serious gaze landed on Elias. "And do you agree with Dr. Turner's diagnosis?"

"I do."

Dr. Wilder's eyes narrowed. "You do?"

"I defer to Dr. Turner's knowledge. I've only

dealt with TTP when I was helping a premature infant. Dr. Turner has seen this more times than I have."

Adeline glanced up at him, a strange look on her face. He hated to admit that he was deferring to his competitor, but Adeline was right, and she understood TTP better, especially when it came to maternal medicine.

"Well, then I'm glad Mrs. Bryant is in your care, Doctors."

"Thank you," Adeline said, seeming stunned at the praise.

"Yes." Dr. Wilder crossed her arms. "You two work well together. I want to keep you as a team for now, because as you know, I only have one spot in my specialty. One. So I want to see how you handle Mrs. Bryant's case. In a month, I have a clinic scheduled in San Francisco, and I want both of you to do the consults there. I know this is a competition, but it would be in your best interests to work together on this."

"Yes, Dr. Wilder," Elias said. "Thank you for the opportunity."

Dr. Wilder nodded. "You both bring unique perspectives, and I want to see how this pans out. You're dismissed."

Adeline turned and walked out of the conference room, and Elias followed. He could tell that she was annoyed and honestly, he couldn't blame her. Dr. Wilder was cold, calculating and tough, but also brilliant.

Still, he was cross that he was stuck working with Adeline too. Especially when he was so tempted being around her. Especially when he could still remember the taste of her lips on his. The last thing he wanted to do was to be forced to work side by side with her.

He needed to put some space between her and him.

It was bad enough they were roommates. He was never going to get away from her.

Is that such a bad thing?

"I can't believe I'm stuck with you!" she said, spinning around.

"Ditto," he grumbled.

She took a step back, and a smiled tweaked her lips. "We're both in agreement: this sucks."

"Yeah, but we have to be professional."

"I'm always professional."

"You weren't so professional last night over dinner," he teased.

Her cheeks bloomed red and she grabbed him by the arm, marching him into an on-call room. She flicked on the lights and shut the door.

Her eyes were wide and he could tell that he'd pushed her too far. She was angry, and so was he.

He needed distance from her, but he was tied to her, just as much as she was tied to him.

Elias was weak when it came to Adeline and he didn't like that one bit.

"Let's get one thing straight. We're not talking about last night," she said hotly.

"Fine."

"It was a mistake that should never have happened."

"You kissed me back too, if I recall." He didn't want to take the entire blame for it. She was just as much to blame as he was, but right now, standing close to her in this on-call room, he couldn't remember the reasons he was angry.

All he could think about was her lips and last night and how he had wished she were someone else—that she wasn't someone he worked with.

You don't get involved with people you work with. Remember that.

It was bad enough that he couldn't go home because Aidan had married his ex, so he certainly wasn't going to have a relationship with someone at work.

Who said anything about a relationship?

Adeline had been so flustered when she had first seen Elias that morning. After their kiss last night, she couldn't get him out of her head. She had wanted that kiss to go further, but she had been too scared.

Too nervous.

She had had short romances, flings, but once

the passion, the attraction, had fizzled out, she had been able to get on with her life.

If she had continued with that kiss, then she could have just moved on.

She'd be over it. She'd be over this attraction she felt for Elias.

Would you?

"I don't like this any more than you, but we have to work together. I'm here to win."

Elias took a step closer and her body trembled, remember how his arms felt around her. "So am I."

Her heart was racing, and she couldn't stop thinking about his kiss.

She had come in here this morning tired and flustered. And when she had seen him in the doctors' lounge, she had felt like she had last night, when she had pushed him away, but really she hadn't wanted to.

She had wanted that kiss to continue.

She wanted to get over this lust, this attraction she felt for her competitor, so that she could get on with her work and focus.

So that she could leave Elias behind.

"You're here to win too?" she asked breathlessly.

"Yes."

Before she could stop herself, she grabbed Elias and pulled him into a kiss, just like last night.

Only this time, she wasn't going to stop.

This time she would get him out of her system. She would get over this lust so that she could go back to what was important.

Her work.

Elias stopped the kiss. "Adeline, are you sure?"

"Yes." She locked the on-call room door, taking his hand, and led him to the bed. "I want you, Elias. And you should know I'm someone who gets what she wants. All I'm asking for is this one time and then we both can focus on our work. I know that you're feeling it too."

"You're right. I am. I can't stop thinking about that kiss, but I can't give you anything more than this."

"I don't want anything more. I don't want a relationship. I just want this moment."

He grinned and pulled her into his arms. "Well, I can't say no to that!"

Elias kissed her again and she melted into his arms.

His kisses were soft, tender, but urgent and full of need, just like she was full of need.

She'd promised him it would just be this one time, but there was a niggling thought in the back of her mind that it could be something more.

It won't be.

This time she wasn't going to stop him.

She needed to have this moment, to get him out of her mind. To clear her head.

She wanted nothing between them. All she wanted was the two of them, skin to skin.

Adeline reached up and began to undo the blue button-down shirt under his scrubs, while he was working on her clothes too.

Too many layers, but at least scrubs were easy to remove.

She couldn't remember the last time she had wanted someone like this. She couldn't recall the last time she had been this aroused.

It was raw.

All-consuming.

It didn't take long before they were both without their clothes. He ran his hands over her body. His touch was like flames, making her moan with need as his fingers found the spot between her thighs.

She was already wet, and she just wanted him to take her.

He ran his tongue over her breasts as he stroked her folds.

"Oh, God," she moaned.

"Yes," he murmured against her neck. "I just want to bury myself inside you, but I need protection." He reached for his wallet and pulled out a condom.

"Here, let me help with that," she purred, taking the packet from him. Then her hands were on him, stroking his length, and he groaned. She smiled secretly as she teased him.

"Oh, God, Adeline."

She kissed him again, pulling him against her. He settled between her legs and thrust into her. She moaned at the feel of him filling her up. It was all she could do to hold back. She wanted him to take her hard and fast.

"Adeline," he murmured against her neck. "What's the rush?"

"I want to come," she panted, kissing him. "Touch me, make me come."

She rolled her hips, urging him to take her.

Faster.

Harder.

Until she cried out, her nails digging in his back as she came around him. It wasn't long until he followed her.

It was like nothing she had ever experienced. Not at this intensity anyway. And it scared her.

"That was great," she whispered, curling up beside him. "Too bad it was just a one-time thing."

"It doesn't have to be. The sex I mean."

Adeline sighed, and even though she didn't want to move, she stood. She had to get away from him, get back to work. She pulled on her scrubs.

"It is just this once, Dr. Garcia."

Elias nodded. "Right. Work, the fellowship and competition."

"Exactly. There's no harm in sleeping with the enemy," she teased, and he laughed.

"Is that what I am? The enemy?"

She slipped on her lab coat. "Yes."

Elias leaned on his elbow and grinned. Still sexy as ever, but he was her rival and she had to a job to do.

And she unlocked the door, slipping out into the hallway.

Maybe now, she could get Elias Garcia out of her head and take the fellowship away from him, because it was hers.

Hers alone.

CHAPTER FIVE

Four weeks later

DR. WILDER WAS going on and on and Adeline tried very hard to focus on what she was saying, but the more she focused, the more she felt like she was going to be sick all over the conference room table.

She was hot and sweaty and had barely slept for the nausea and indigestion that had plagued her all night for the last couple of nights.

"Dr. Turner," Dr. Wilder said, breaking through Adeline's cloud of thoughts.

"Yes." Adeline sat up straight, fighting another wave of nausea.

"Mrs. Bryant's baby's lung maturity and gestational age are far enough along to safely deliver. Today we're going to deliver it. I need you to prep her for surgery and let her know the risks given her TTP diagnosis."

Adeline nodded. "Yes, Dr. Wilder."

"I'll be in the operating room, but this is your

patient. You're the lead surgeon on this C-section and possible hysterectomy. Dr. Garcia will assist and then take the lead on the baby's welfare once the baby is delivered."

"Thank you, Dr. Wilder," Elias said, glancing at Adeline with concern.

Although she really didn't need his pity.

For the last month the two of them had been working on Mrs. Bryant's case and assisting Dr. Wilder with her other patients.

Adeline had worked to keep one step ahead of Elias, but lately she'd been completely under the weather, and to her frustration, Elias was doing more work than her.

The only saving grace was that Elias was easy to work with. And as much as she had dreaded his arrival at SDMH at first, now she was glad he was here.

It had been a bumpy start, especially with that one mistake—the moment of passion—but there was no other surgeon in the OB-GYN specialty that she'd rather work with.

Elias was talented.

So she did not need him looking at her with concern and pity.

She had some kind of bug. Nothing more. She just had to shake it.

After this meeting she was going to do a blood draw. She had to find out what had been making her sick. In two days she was flying out to San

Francisco with Elias to work on consults for Dr. Wilder. She didn't have time to be ill.

Maybe you're not sick. Maybe you're pregnant?

And she laughed to herself at that thought. It was absurd. She and Elias had used protection. It couldn't be pregnancy. It just couldn't.

Her stomach twisted and knotted. All she could think about was the women she'd seen over the years who had gotten pregnant while using protection.

The blood drained from her face. She needed a blood test. Right away.

"Okay, everyone. You have your duties. Let's prep Mrs. Bryant for surgery."

Everyone started to leave, but Adeline remained behind to catch her breath, because the room was spinning. Terror at the thought that she might be pregnant overtook her. Her pulse was thundering in her ears and she couldn't focus.

What if she were pregnant?

Part of her would be secretly thrilled because she had always wanted a family, but then all she could think about was her mother and what had happened to her.

The idea of losing her child was too much to bear, and tears welled up in her eyes for a brief moment.

She brushed them away.

She didn't want anyone to see her cry.

She glanced up and saw Elias staring at her, concerned.

Adeline's cheeks heated and she felt embarrassed that he had caught her crying.

"Adeline, are you okay?" Elias asked gently.

"What?"

"You zoned out and you look awful."

"I feel awful." Adeline buried her head in her elbow on the table. "Not that it's your business." Then she felt bad for snapping at him. She looked up at him and saw he was worried.

She couldn't remember the last time someone had asked her how she was feeling.

It was nice.

Elias sighed. "No, it's not my business, but you've been sick for a week. It's no fun without you on my ass giving me heat."

Adeline chuckled. "I did swabs for COVID because I'm working in the operating room. It's negative. I've been testing for other things. Nothing is conclusive."

Elias's brow furrowed. "Well, if you want, we can run a blood test and look for a bunch of stuff. I doubt TTP because I'm sure you've been running your blood pressure."

"It's elevated. No signs of purpura though." Adeline groaned.

"See, this is why you should get genetic testing done. Your mother's TTP was genetic, right?"

Adeline sighed. "I did. I got it done after we

were together, but it'll take some time for it to track down the gene. Gene sequencing takes a while."

"Did you do an ADAMTS13 as well when you did the draw for the genetic test?" he asked.

"No, the ADAMTS13 smear looks for deformities in the red blood cell. My blood test is to check if I have the gene for the inherited version of TTP. I wasn't having symptoms, so the smear wouldn't have shown anything. A month ago, I had no signs to warrant the ADAMTS13 smear. Now that I have some symptoms, I need to check if there are deformities in my red blood cells."

Elias looked impressed. "Good for you. I'm glad you saw sense."

She sighed. "Do my blood test so I can get to work. I can't let whatever this is derail me. You can do an ADAMTS13 smear now if you'd like."

"You're probably worn out. We've been busy this past month."

Adeline stood and followed Elias out of the conference room. He was right. Dr. Wilder had kept them busy.

Dr. Wilder liked their pairing and partnered them up. A lot. So much that Adeline was kind of getting used to working with him.

"Take a seat," Elias ordered as he got everything ready to take her blood.

"You know it will tick me off if it's just exhaustion," she muttered.

"Why's that?" he asked, casually swabbing her arm with alcohol.

"Because you've been working the same hours and still look good. What's with men?"

Elias grinned. "You're such a complainer. I won't miss that when I win the spot with Dr. Wilder."

"Ha ha." Adeline winced as the needle pricked her.

"There." Elias finished up. "Hold that cotton ball tight. Honestly, just this blood draw should show signs of TTP. Especially with the AD-AMTS13 smear done."

"I know."

Elias bagged the vial of blood for the lab and then leaned closer to her, making her heart beat faster.

She could still recall his touch on her skin, the feel of his lips on her body.

The pleasure he had brought to her. Even though they had been together a month ago, she still thought about it. Every once in a while when they were working together, she'd look up and see him there, smiling at her. She'd get a rush, a zing of heat, and recall how it had felt to be in his arms.

It was distracting.

She'd hoped their one night together would be enough, but it hadn't been.

She wanted more, but she wasn't going to give in.

Once with the enemy was enough.

"You worry too much," he whispered and kissed her gently.

That kiss brought back the flush of heat. Her heart beat a bit faster. She forgot that he had just drawn her blood and she'd been sick for a week.

His gentle kiss made her feel safe.

Like it was going to be okay, and that frightened her.

She didn't want him to make her feel safe.

"Elias," she murmured.

"What?" he teased.

"You don't need to be so concerned. I'm fine." She hoped she wasn't blushing too much.

"Don't I? You're sick."

"I'm fine. Besides, you have the upper hand, being well. You can get more work done."

He chuckled. "I know, but I'm worried about you. This is not like you."

Adeline nodded. "Tell me about it."

"We'd better get Mrs. Bryant ready for surgery," he said, standing up instead of leaning over her again. "I'll get this to the lab and put a rush on it."

"Thanks." Adeline removed the cotton ball, looking for signs of extensive bruising, but there was nothing. She placed a bandage over it. "And thanks again for being there."

"That's what friends are for." He turned and left, taking her blood work to the lab.

Adeline sighed, because although she was glad they were still colleagues, perhaps even friends, after their passionate encounter, a part of her wanted more.

And the wanting more always got her into trouble.

Always.

Elias was on the opposite side of the operating table and he was watching Adeline like a hawk. She seemed to be handling the surgery well, but there were times during the prepping of Mrs. Bryant when she'd looked a little green around the gills.

Dr. Wilder hovered and watched over the both of them like a hawk too.

Elias was getting tired of Dr. Wilder pairing him and Adeline together, especially when she would eventually break them up.

Why create a surgical team to end it?

Only one of them could get the position.

And it was going to be him.

He wanted to prove to Dr. Wilder he was a good solo surgeon, but that was hard to do when Dr. Wilder insisted he work with Adeline all the time.

It was grating on his nerves.

You came here to learn from the best.

He had to keep reminding himself of that.

Even though he really liked working with Adeline.

Still, it was his fellowship.

No one was going to get in his way.

The only person he could rely on, the only person he could trust, was himself. Everyone else was a disappointment.

He had trusted Shea and she had broken his heart. He had trusted Aidan and Aidan had stabbed him in the back by stealing Shea, marrying her and being the golden son of Garcia Estates Winery.

Don't think of them.

Nothing he had ever done was good enough.

But when he became just as world-renowned as Dr. Wilder, maybe his father would respect his choices. Maybe then he could make his father proud. His throat constricted as he tried not to think about his father.

How he could never do anything right.

He was tired of feeling less than.

Instead he thought of Adeline, and he couldn't help but smile to himself. Everything else melted away as he thought of her tender kisses, the way she'd sighed in his arms, the scent of her skin and the silkiness of her hair.

It made him think about how much he wanted those moments back, even briefly.

How much he still wanted her in his arms. And it scared him.

"Dr. Garcia, are you ready to deliver the baby?" Adeline asked, breaking through his thoughts.

"Yes, Dr. Turner."

The baby had been experiencing intermittent late and variable decelerations the longer Mrs. Bryant's treatment for the TTP went on.

They had bumped the surgery to save the baby.

Elias reached down and gently removed the tiny little boy.

"You have a son," Elias said to Mrs. Bryant, who was awake. He carried the boy to the incubator to clear his lungs.

"How is he?" Mrs. Bryant asked. "I don't hear a cry. Oh, God."

"It's okay, Mrs. Bryant," Adeline gently said. "They're clearing his lungs. He's in good hands with Dr. Garcia."

Elias worked quickly and soon there was a gasp, the intake of that first breath of life, and a small cry.

He smiled, never getting tired of that moment. "There we go. Good boy."

He could hear Mr. and Mrs. Bryant both crying with joy. Elias finished his tests on the newborn and brought the boy over to his parents.

"Congratulations on your son. He's needing some extra oxygen, so we're going to take him to the NICU. Mr. Bryant, you can accompany your son if you'd like."

Mr. Bryant looked at his wife and she nodded.

Elias carried the boy and helped the NICU team get the baby in the incubator.

He would check on the baby later, but right now he had to stay and assist Adeline. Elias changed gloves and came back to the table.

Adeline was working quickly, but the damage was too great. Mrs. Bryant was bleeding too much and the treatment for the clots meant she was bleeding out.

An alarm sounded.

"She's crashing. We're going to intubate," the anesthesiologist said.

"Dammit," Adeline cursed under her breath.

Dr. Wilder stepped forward. "What's the next step, Dr. Turner?"

"Hysterectomy." Adeline shook her head. "There's too much damage. The patient understood this might happen."

Elias worked with Adeline as a crash C-section turned into a hysterectomy.

There was no choice. The damage the blood clots had caused was too great and part of the placenta had begun to rupture.

They had saved the baby's life in the nick of time. Now it was time to save the mother's.

Elias marveled at Adeline's skill. Especially since he knew she was under the weather. And he decided right there that if he lost the spot to Adeline, it would be worth it. He wouldn't be upset if he lost to her.

She was a worthy opponent.

So are you.

No matter what his father thought of him, he was a surgeon.

A respected one.

This was his dream. And nothing would stand in his way.

Not even Adeline.

The surgery took a bit longer, but soon they were done. Mrs. Bryant was stable, and Dr. Wilder was happy.

Elias scrubbed out next to Adeline. "How are you feeling?"

"Beat," Adeline murmured as she rolled her shoulders.

"You did great."

"Thanks. I'm glad everyone is okay. Now we see if the symptoms of TTP goes away or if the patient has the genetic version and will have flare-ups."

Elias nodded.

"Dr. Garcia?"

He turned to see an intern hovering in the scrub room door.

"Yes?" he asked.

"Lab results." The intern handed him the paper.

He dried his hands and took the sheet. The intern left and he saw it was Adeline's blood work.

"Your results."

Adeline sighed. "Read it to me."

"You sure?"

She nodded. "My eyes are so blurry I don't think I can. You do it."

Elias scanned the paper. "ADAMTS13 is negative. Red blood cells are fine."

Adeline sighed again. "Great."

He could hear the relief in her voice. He continued to read through the negative results and then his heart stopped beating when he saw the hCG level.

Pregnant?

"Elias, what's wrong? You're freaking me out."

"You're pregnant, Adeline," Elias murmured, in shock. "You're pregnant with my baby."

Adeline couldn't believe what she was hearing. The room began to spin and it felt like she was free-falling without a parachute.

"I've got to go." She didn't know where, but she had to put some space between her, Elias and the news that had hit her hard on the head like a sledgehammer.

"Adeline, where are you going?" Elias asked, falling into step beside her.

"Back to my rounds." She laughed to herself. "You're completely pulling my leg."

"No. I'm not." Elias looked dead serious, which made her pause and take the lab report from him, her hands trembling.

And there it was.

A lab report didn't lie. She was actually pregnant with Elias's child.

And all she could think about was that she had made another huge mistake and Elias was going to use this pregnancy against her to get the fellowship.

She watched her career just crumble before her.

What have I done?

"I don't feel so good," she murmured, and she could feel the blood draining from her face. Elias's arm went around her, and he quickly led her out of the main hallway into a dark exam room.

"Here, lie down." He gently moved her to the examination table. He didn't turn on the lights, which was fine. There was some sunlight peeking in through the blinds at the window. "Breathe deeply."

"I am. Trust me," she muttered.

He wet a paper towel and held it to her head. He was being so sweet again. It was scary that he was seeing her like this.

Weak.

Scared.

All things he could use against her.

He's not Gregory.

Still, it was hard to trust him. Trust that he'd be around for their baby or that he wouldn't use this to his advantage.

And though she was thrilled on some level to be pregnant, she was terrified of what this was going to mean for her chance at the spot. When she was first asked to compete for the fellowship, Dr. Wilder had made it very clear that it was a grueling four years.

She had spelled out, in no uncertain terms, that there was no time for a personal life.

So how was having a baby going to look? The worst part of it was, her direct competition was the person who had knocked her up. She felt like she was going to be sick.

"What're we going to do?" she asked.

"What do you mean?"

"What do you mean, what do I mean? We're going to have a baby. It's your baby too. Or was that your master plan to take me out of the picture?"

Elias crossed his arms. "I'm not some kind of villain."

"We're going to have a baby." She was in shock. And she couldn't help but smile.

It was scary, but it wasn't a bad thing. Just really poorly timed.

"I know," he said gently. "Truth be told, I have no clue what to do. I suppose we could get married."

Adeline snorted. "What? This isn't the 1950s. We don't have to get married."

"Yeah, I know. I didn't realize how silly that sounded." He smiled the half smile that made her weak at the knees. "Well, I'm going to be here for both of you. I want you to know that. We can raise this baby together. You might be doing all the hard work now, but I'll always be there for you. That you have my word on."

"I don't want to tell anyone," she said, her voice trembling. "Please don't tell anyone."

"People will eventually find out."

Her heart sank.

"Are you going to tell them, though?" she asked, forcing the words out.

"No, but eventually you'll show." Elias made a gesture, holding his hand out, his eyes twinkling.

Adeline smiled. "You're right."

"I won't say anything."

She looked into his eyes, and she wanted to trust him, but Gregory had lied to her.

How could she trust Elias?

"Dr. Wilder is making her announcement soon. I don't want my pregnancy to cloud her judgment," she whispered.

Elias cocked an eyebrow. "And what happens if you get it and then Dr. Wilder finds out about your pregnancy?"

"You can't discriminate against a pregnant woman," she said quickly.

Elias shook his head. "She can't do that now."

"She might!" Adeline sat up. "Ignore me, I'm being irrational."

"It's okay. It's a lot to take in. Trust me." He sighed, running his hand through his hair, making his curls stand on end. "Like I said, I won't say anything."

"You won't?"

Elias expression softened and he touched her face. "I won't."

She wanted to believe him.

I'm not married, Gregory had said. *Why do you want to know? We're having a good time. That's all that matters.*

Adeline shook the thought out of her head. She'd fallen for Gregory's smile and charming words. She didn't want to make the same mistake again.

Elias is different. You can trust him.

"I need you to do something else."

"Oh?" he asked cautiously.

"I need you to monitor me for signs of TTP. The genetic test still hasn't come in and… I'm worried."

"But we ran your blood work, you're okay, and now we know why your BP was raised."

"Elias, please." She hated to beg, but she was terrified. All she could think of was her mother. All she could remember was the anxiety that had permeated the air when her mother had fallen pregnant again or when her mother had had a flare-up.

Tears stung her eyes and she was angry at herself for crying. Especially in front of Elias. She didn't cry in front of anyone.

She never let anyone see her tears, but she couldn't stop them from coming. She was losing control and she hated it.

What was wrong with her?

You're pregnant.

"Hey, don't worry. We'll watch it. I promise, but I don't think it's something you have."

"And if it is?" she asked.

"We'll deal with it." Elias put an arm around her and held her close. Part of her wanted to push him away, but she didn't. Instead she curled up against him and tried to regain control of her emotions, which were all over the place. She felt so safe with his arm around her. Like he would never let her go, like she could happily stay here, wrapped up in his arm forever.

Only, the other part of her was scared that he'd leave her.

And it would be just her and the baby.

This was the part of her that reminded her there was no forever with Elias.

How could there be?

Tears really began to flow then. She hated the way she was losing control over her feelings. She was scared of picturing any kind of happy-ever-after with Elias.

She had a hard time believing he'd be around for this baby.

The only other time she'd ever pictured some sort of happy-ever-after was when she was with Gregory, and look how that had turned out.

He had lied to her. He'd been married. He'd made a fool of her.

And then because she had dumped him when she found out he was married, he had said she was the one who came on to him because she wanted good grades, all so he could save his job.

Adeline had been duped back then and had sworn that she was never going to let that happen again, so she had let go of her romantic dreams and focused on what she could control.

"Well, we'd better go find Dr. Wilder. See what our next case is." She shrugged out of his side hug and stood up, wiping her face.

"Are you going to be okay?"

"No," she said. "But I will be, and I'll still kick your butt. Especially when we're in San Francisco."

Elias smiled at her and nodded. "We'll be okay. We've got this. We're a good team and we're good competitors."

He was right. They were, but how long would they be?

That was the question.

Only one of them was going to walk away with the position. And if it was Elias, would he even have time for the baby that he had conceived during a one-night stand?

They found Dr. Wilder in her office.

"How is the patient doing?" Dr. Wilder asked.

"Stable," Adeline answered. "I sent you my operative report, which I typed up right after I scrubbed out."

Dr. Wilder nodded. "Thank you. You did very well. Both of you did. How is the infant doing, Dr. Garcia?"

"The baby boy is also stable. He's on a nasal cannula for oxygen but is otherwise fine. He scored an Apgar of three when born and now is a seven in the NICU. He's responding quite well."

Dr. Wilder nodded again. "Good. Remember that you were going to San Francisco in a couple of days to run consults? I need you two to go tonight."

"Tonight?" Elias asked.

"Yes. There is a patient currently admitted. She is pregnant with twins. The head of obstetrics is my friend and he's a bit short-staffed. He could use some help and you two are the best. You're a good team and balance each other well. I'd like to fly you up to San Francisco tonight. Everything will be paid for."

"Thank you, Dr. Wilder," Adeline said. "I am definitely interested in the challenge."

"Yes," Elias said, hoping his voice didn't show his uncertainty. He'd been dreaming about this trip since Dr. Wilder had announced it.

He had been trying to figure out a way to get out of it.

Only he couldn't. Not if he wanted the fellowship. "Thank you."

"Good. Well, get home and pack up. The Hospital for Special Surgery in San Francisco is sending their private jet to pick you both up. The flight leaves at seven."

Adeline turned and left the office, and Elias followed her out.

He didn't want to go to San Francisco.

Elias's mind was still reeling over Adeline's test result. He was going to be a father and that shocked him.

It was something he had always wanted but hadn't expected to happen.

And certainly not now.

And not with Adeline.

Pregnant.

They had used protection, but the logical part of his brain reminded him that protection wasn't infallible.

A family had never been his plan after Shea had left him and embarrassed him by marrying Aidan. He just couldn't put his heart on the line to commit to someone else. But even though it wasn't part of his plan, he wasn't going to abandon this baby or Adeline.

This was his child and he was going to be there for the baby. No matter what and no matter who got the position. Adeline didn't believe it, but Elias was a man of his word.

He would not tell anyone about this baby until Adeline was ready and he would not abandon it if he got the job. He was a bit nervous about being in San Francisco, so close to home. So close to his family.

He hadn't seen them in two years. They had been texting him, emailing him a lot, especially his sister, but Elias had kept putting them off.

He wasn't ready to go back, and he wasn't in the right frame of mind to deal with his family. He didn't want to go back until he had this fellowship. If they knew he was in San Francisco working, he'd have no excuse not to see them. They'd come to San Francisco just to visit him.

Well, at least his sister and mother would.

Elias wasn't so sure about his father and younger brother.

"You okay?" Adeline asked. "Now you seem to be a bit catatonic."

"It's been a lot today," he muttered. "And honestly, I don't want to go to San Francisco."

"Why? I thought you were excited about this consult?"

"I was, but San Francisco is close to Napa."

"And your family."

"I've been dreading this since Dr. Wilder mentioned it, but there was no way out of it. Part of me hoped it would be canceled."

Adeline smiled. "Instead it was bumped up."

Elias sighed. "I've been avoiding my family for two years."

Adeline's eyes widened. "Whoa, all because you didn't take over the family estate."

"Partly, but mostly because…" He trailed off. "My brother married my ex."

And he couldn't believe he was telling Adeline that. Something about her relaxed him and let him put down his guard. He had never told anyone about his brother stealing his ex. It was his burden to bear.

And it made him nervous that Adeline had broken down his walls.

That he told her about his shame, that Shea didn't think he was worthy enough, but Aidan was.

You grew apart.

Still, Aidan had always needed to have what Elias had. Except Aidan hadn't been able to compete with Elias when it came to academics. Aidan hadn't made the grades to go to a university. He hadn't gotten the awards or scholarships.

And Elias knew it had driven Aidan crazy.

Did it, though?

That thought gave Elias pause. Maybe he'd rubbed his scholarships and his awards in Aidan's face too much over the years. Aidan had a knack for the vineyard. He liked being out there on the land and Elias didn't. That wasn't a bad thing.

Still, Aidan had Shea and had their father's admiration.

"That's kind of messed up," Adeline said, interrupting his thoughts.

And he chuckled. "Right?"

"Well, don't tell them you're in San Francisco. We're there to work. We're going to be busy."

He nodded. "Yeah."

"I have a few things to finish here and then I'm headed back to the beach house to pack. I have a feeling we're going to be in San Francisco for a few days. We can share a ride to the airport."

"Okay. I'll see you later."

Adeline smiled and walked away, but Elias didn't feel any relief. He was cross because he had told her that secret part about him.

He hated sharing that, and it scared him how easy it was being around Adeline. How easy it was to open up to her.

It was dangerous, but for the first time in a long while, it didn't sting as much to think of Shea and Aidan.

It's because of Adeline. It's because of the baby.

And that thought terrified him too. His last real

relationship had been Shea, but Adeline had gotten under his skin.

And he cared for her.

And he was really happy about the baby.

Scared, but thrilled.

He was going to absolutely be there for the baby, but Adeline had made it clear she didn't want him. She didn't want marriage. She just wanted to remain as they were. For the first time in a long time, all Elias could think of was that he was so close to having everything he had dreamed about when he was younger. When he'd been planning his life with Shea.

Of course, the family was to come after his career was secure. Only, now he wasn't sure he would be able to claim it.

He was afraid his old dreams of having a family would be snatched away, like so many of his dreams in the past had been.

CHAPTER SIX

IT FELT SO good to be home.

Her life was in turmoil at the moment: the fellowship, her pregnancy and these few days of consults in San Francisco. Everything was crazy, but it still felt good to be back.

It had been a long time since Adeline had been in San Francisco. It hadn't been two years like Elias, but still, it had been a good six months since she'd been to see her parents, and though she wanted to go see her mother while she was here, she wasn't sure.

Mom would find out about the pregnancy, and Adeline really didn't want to trigger something in her or make her worried, especially when Adeline didn't even have the results of that genetic test.

It was already bothering her enough, the not knowing, but logically she knew how long genetic testing took.

She also didn't want her mother to get her hopes up about a wedding or some kind of fairytale happily-ever-after for Adeline.

Wouldn't that be nice, though?

She smiled to herself thinking of that, but it wasn't going to happen.

Adeline was also worried about the bad timing of this whole pregnancy. At least she wasn't showing yet and only Elias knew about it.

No one else had to know yet, and other than her obvious morning sickness, she was okay.

Elias didn't say much on the flight up to San Francisco. He was brooding the whole way and she couldn't blame him. Not after what he had told her. They had both been sharing a lot. It was kind of nice to talk to someone about things.

To trust someone enough to share.

Adeline hadn't realized how lonely she'd been.

Still, she didn't like anyone knowing about her personal problems, so it put them on equal ground with her knowing about his family. Adeline was fine with not talking. She really didn't have a whole lot to say either.

She had her own worries. She didn't need to trouble him.

As long as Elias kept his word and didn't tell Dr. Wilder about her pregnancy.

He had promised he wouldn't, and she wanted to believe him.

She really did. Only, there was a part of her that wouldn't let her.

She took a deep breath and tried to calm her nerves.

But she was so scared. So scared of losing it all: the baby, the fellowship and Elias.

That thought took her by surprise because she didn't have Elias.

They were friends now, colleagues, but he wasn't hers and she wasn't his.

After the plane landed, they were whisked away to a two-bedroom apartment that the hospital owned for visiting physicians. It was located near the Panhandle district, which was close to the Botanical Gardens and Golden Gate Park.

She was across town from her parents, who lived in Cow Hollow.

Well, not completely across town, but it would take a few connections on the bus to get from the Panhandle district to Cow Hollow, which was down near the Presidio.

The apartment was furnished sparsely, but it would be comfortable enough for them. Suddenly she was nervous about being alone with Elias in this apartment. Even though they lived together as roommates in San Diego, her room was on a different floor than Elias's.

And James and Sherrie were there too. They were buffers.

This was different. This was just the two of them. Alone.

She was more nervous than she had thought.

"This is nicer than I expected," Elias remarked as he wandered around the modern apartment furnished in grays and whites, with floor-to-ceiling windows in the living room, which faced the park. So there was a nice view of the green trees that covered the Panhandle. "So different from sand and the beach."

"I know. I forgot how much I missed trees that weren't palm trees," she teased.

"San Diego has other trees."

"Yeah, but it's more arid." Adeline wandered into one of the bedrooms and sank down on the king-sized bed. Her room had its own bathroom. It was a bit nicer than her place in the beach house.

"You look comfortable." Elias leaned against the door jamb.

"I am," Adeline remarked, sighing. "It's been a long day."

"Are you hungry? I thought we might walk somewhere and get something to eat?"

She should have said no, kept her distance, and she was tired. But she was hungry.

Her stomach won out over her need to sleep.

"That sounds good."

His phone vibrated and he pulled it out of his pocket, frowning when he saw the text, before slipping it away.

"Your family?" Adeline asked.

"It's like they have radar and know when to start hassling me. They know that I left my previous internship in Houston and am back in California, in San Diego."

"How did they find that out?" she asked.

Elias sighed. "I told my nephew, and now my sister is threatening to drive down to San Diego to see me."

"That would be a long, disappointing drive," Adeline teased.

"It would."

"You could say you're unavailable."

"She'd still drive down to see me."

"You might as well tell her where you are but tell her you're busy."

"I will, but first, let's go get something to eat before all the restaurants close. We have a busy day tomorrow with that patient, consults and whatever else comes our way." He was counting on his fingers, his eyes twinkling, and he was back to the same easygoing Elias she'd grown to know over the last month.

Adeline laughed. "Fine."

She grabbed her purse and they headed out of their apartment and down the stairs to the street. It took her a moment to orient herself, but soon they were walking on Masonic Avenue, across the park towards Haight-Ashbury. Haight Street was lined with various places to dine.

They settled on a little Mexican place that had a rooftop patio, so they could enjoy the cool evening breeze of San Francisco.

And so they could talk, because the inside of the restaurant was packed full of people and had blaring Mexican music, making it impossible to hear anything.

"I am glad I brought my sweater," Adeline said, pulling on her cardigan.

"It is nice tonight. Not that San Diego is overly hot either in June. I find the fall the hottest time of the year."

"Yes. Especially here too."

"So if it's June, our baby should be born… in February?" Elias was counting on his fingers again and Adeline was chuckling. "What's so funny?"

"You count on your fingers."

He looked down. "It's something I picked up when I was a kid. I can do math quickly in my head when it comes to things like medicating and measurements, but since I was a kid I've counted on my fingers."

"I think it's cute." And then heat bloomed in her cheeks, and she was embarrassed she'd said that out loud. There was a lot about Elias that she liked. And a lot that made her nervous.

No one had ever made her feel like this before.

Not even Gregory.

She had been hoping their time together a month ago had been enough to get him out of her system, but it had done the exact opposite. She liked being around him. She liked working with him. He was charming, funny, sexy and easy to talk to. And now she was pregnant with his baby and she couldn't get him out of her mind. She kept thinking about all the what-ifs.

And that scared her.

She was afraid of getting hurt again.

"Thanks, I think." He winked and smiled. "So, am I right about March?"

"Yes. Based on my last cycle, I'm thinking around St. Patrick's Day. If everything goes normally." She crossed her fingers.

"Why are you crossing your fingers?"

"I don't want to jinx it." She sighed. "I want it all to work out."

"I had no idea you were superstitious."

"I'm not."

He cocked an eyebrow and looked at her in disbelief. "Really?"

"Fine. I am. I'm a surgeon, I have a scientific mind and I have some superstitions."

"And I think that's cute," he whispered, making her heart skip a beat. "Besides, most surgeons you'll find are superstitious. They may not want to admit it, but there are certain things that surgeons do to bring about the good vibes."

"And what do you do?"

He grinned, those dark eyes of his twinkling again. "I count on my fingers."

Adeline blushed again, thinking how cute he was when he did that, just as the waiter came over to take their order. As much as she really wanted to have a big tequila-laden margarita, she resisted and opted for the alcohol-free version and chicken mole.

She was craving beef, the rarer the better, but she knew that wasn't safe for the baby.

Elias opted for iced tea and an enchilada.

"You know, you can have a beer or something," she said.

"No. I'm okay with iced tea. I want my wits about me for tomorrow and it was a long day—Mrs. Bryant's surgery, our little news and flying up to San Francisco." The way he said *San Francisco* was in disgust or annoyance.

"It's really bothering you to be back here?"

He nodded. "I decided to text my sister and tell her that I was in San Francisco this weekend, but I was working and wouldn't have time to see her. She hasn't responded, but at least she won't be driving down to San Diego, searching the streets for me."

"She cares about you. It's sweet."

"And what about your family? You said they were in San Francisco. Are you going to make time to see them?"

Adeline sighed. "I suppose I must."

"Now who's avoiding seeing their family?" he teased.

"I'm not avoiding them…well, I am, sort of. I don't want to worry my mom or tell her I'm pregnant until we have the results of the genetic testing."

"Well, you can still see her. She won't know you're pregnant."

Adeline nodded. "True, but she'll know that I'm off. I can't hide anything from her."

"What about...your brother, was it?"

"He's married with kids and lives in Oakland, across the bay. He's pretty busy, but I'll text him and let him know I'm here. I haven't seen my two nephews in a couple of months. It would be nice to see them again."

"How old are they?"

"Five. They're twins." She smiled. "Twins run in my family."

His eyes widened. "They run in mine too. We'd better get you an ultrasound sooner rather than later!"

Adeline laughed out loud. "Could you imagine?"

And then the thought hit her harder.

What if it is twins?

"Oh, my God," she whispered. "That would be..."

She tried to picture herself with two babies and saw two dark-haired little girls, and the thought gave her a secret thrill.

"Difficult!" Elias said, finishing her sentence and interrupting her thoughts.

They both laughed at the absurdity of that, because it was too early for an ultrasound to determine whether or not there was one baby or two or more, and wouldn't it just figure? Knowing her luck.

Yet there was a part of her that wanted it to happen.

So badly.

A family.

"Cross your fingers again, Adeline. And keep them crossed so it's just one," Elias teased.

"I'll keep everything crossed from now on," Adeline muttered.

He winked. "Well, not everything."

Heat rushed through her veins. She hoped that she wasn't blushing and if she was, she hoped he couldn't see it in the dim light of the rooftop patio.

It was supposed to be a one-time thing.

She didn't want a relationship. Especially when one of them would have to lose for the other to take the fellowship. Only, they were friends now. They were sharing this baby.

She felt hot and bothered as she looked at him, her heart racing, her stomach fluttering with anticipation as she thought of that time a month ago and how good it had felt to be in his arms.

There was a part of her that said it couldn't hurt. She was already pregnant.

Her conflicting thoughts were interrupted when the waiter brought their food, and for the first time in a month, Adeline didn't feel sick at the sight or smell of food.

She just hoped her body didn't change its mind later.

"So, neonatology. That's a difficult specialty. Why did you choose it?" she asked, making casual conversation.

Elias cocked an eyebrow. The dimple on his cheek nearly made her swoon.

"Getting to know the competition better?"

"I think we're beyond that."

"Are we?" he asked.

Her cheeks flushed. "Well, we're still competitors, but tonight…tonight we can be friends."

"I'd like that. For tonight." He winked.

"So?"

"So?"

"Why neonatology and medicine instead of vineyards?"

Elias sighed. "Well, besides me being a preemie, like I said, my nephew, Manny, was born early and almost died. I was fifteen years old and decided then and there to be a NICU doctor. I was never interested in the vineyard. Much to my father's disappointment." He shrugged. "Medicine is my passion. It's never let me down."

Adeline understood that.

Medicine had never let her down either.

"So, how about you? Was it just your mother's

TTP that drove you to this fellowship or do you have something to prove like me?"

He meant it as a tease, but he was right. She had something to prove.

"I changed medical schools due to a personal issue. One that almost wrecked my career, so yeah, I have something to prove."

He raised his eyebrows. "Oh?"

"I got involved with the wrong man. That's all I'm going to say."

And she had said too much already.

Why was it so easy to spill too much information to him? How did he get under her skin? What was it about him?

She had to be more careful. Although she trusted him more than she had ever trusted anyone before, she still couldn't be completely sure of him.

She was too scared.

They had an enjoyable dinner and Adeline footed the bill because she still hadn't paid Elias back for that evening when he ordered in pad thai, which had led to that kiss, which had led to the on-call room the next day, which had led to their current predicament. It was late and they both had an early morning meeting with their respective teams and getting to know the patients.

Adeline was looking forward to throwing herself into her work and trying not to think about her pregnancy, her family or Elias.

Although she was working closely with him, so she couldn't completely put him out of her mind.

She knew this feeling well.

It had been some time since she had experienced anything like this, but she was falling for Elias. And she was annoyed with herself for falling for the wrong man.

Again.

She was falling for her rival. Falling for a man she might end up hurting if she got the fellowship over him.

Or vice versa.

She had a feeling this was doomed and that thought saddened her.

It doesn't have to be this way.

Only she was having a hard time convincing herself that it would be okay.

She was so afraid of opening her heart and trusting again.

"You okay?" he asked as they walked back to the apartment in silence.

"I am. Just tired." Which wasn't a lie. She was exhausted, both physically and mentally. It had been a long day.

She had to get control over her emotions, which was hard to do being pregnant, but she had to. She wasn't going to get hurt again.

She couldn't.

Her heart couldn't take it.

Especially not where Elias Garcia was concerned. He meant too much to her. She didn't want their friendship to end.

She didn't want her baby's—their baby's—parents to hate each other.

Over what? A job?

For the sake of the baby, she had to be careful.

Elias tossed and turned all night.

All he could think about was the texts from his sister, wanting to see him. Hurt that he hadn't texted her sooner to let her know that he had moved from Houston to San Diego. And even though he didn't want to drive to Napa, he was going to have to at some point.

There was no getting around it. He'd put it off too long.

And he hated the fact that he would be going there empty-handed.

He didn't have the fellowship yet. He didn't own his own place. He still had roommates. He didn't have a serious relationship. He was showing no sign of settling down, which was what his dad valued as success. Elias had none of those things.

Nothing to prove to them that his education had been worth it.

Nothing tangible for them except Adeline carrying his child. His parents would be thrilled about the baby, but his father would ask him why he wasn't with Adeline.

He'd ask why they weren't together.

Why they weren't married.

His father would just complain that Elias could never settle down.

He'd complain that he wandered around from school to school, job to job, woman to woman.

It was his wandering that had caused him to drift apart from Shea. Although he had never cheated on her, he had grown emotionally apart from Shea, which had allowed Aidan to swoop in and take her.

Aidan had always wanted what Elias had, and though he hadn't made the grades to go to medical school, Aidan had gotten the girl, the vineyard and their father's approval.

Elias had one thing Aidan didn't. A medical degree. And soon a fellowship.

But not Adeline.

And that thought made him sad.

Only one of them would win this fellowship.

And what would his father think if he took it from the mother of his child? The fellowship wouldn't matter to his father. His father would be ashamed and honestly, so would Elias.

So why should he even go back home?

Aidan would be right there, rubbing in how he'd done all the right things and Elias had made a mess of his life.

What he wanted to do was take Adeline there, show her off as his significant other and tell them all she was pregnant. He liked Adeline and he was thrilled about the baby.

He wanted to prove to them that his life was together. They didn't understand that becoming a surgeon took time; that he wasn't throwing his life away because of it.

Cursing under his breath, he threw off the covers and pulled on his jeans, so he wouldn't scare Adeline walking around naked.

Although he had the distinct feeling that it wouldn't freak her out too much. And that thought made him smile and laugh softly to himself.

He crept down the hall and checked her room, but she wasn't there, which made him worried. He headed out to the living room and she was standing at the window, staring out at the darkness.

"Adeline?" he asked.

She turned around. "I couldn't sleep. I'm nervous about tomorrow and every time I get nervous, I feel a bit nauseated. Why are you up?"

"I couldn't sleep either. I was thinking about…" He trailed off, running his hand through his hair. "Thinking about tomorrow as well."

Which was the half-truth.

Adeline sighed and sat down on the couch, and he sat down next to her.

"What are we going to do?" she asked.

"About what?"

"About the baby and who gets the fellowship. Only one of us can get the fellowship."

His stomach twisted. "I don't know."

"I hate this. I never thought I'd say it, but I hate this fellowship."

"Me too."

"So?".

"What do we do?" he asked gently.

"Yeah."

"Like I said, I don't know."

"That's not very reassuring," she teased.

"Okay. You want reassuring. We try to sleep and we get up and do our jobs. We don't think about all the solutions right now. We take this one day at a time and do the best that we can do for those patients."

"You're right." She sighed and leaned up against him on the couch. It was nice having her so close. It was nice holding her here on the couch. He could smell the lavender scent of her shampoo and he reached out to touch her soft, silky hair.

She snuggled in closer.

He liked this.

Being with her.

It felt right. It was nice not competing right now.

"I'm always right," he teased. He should get up and leave, but he didn't want to move.

"Whoever gets the fellowship, we'll figure it out." She yawned. "We'll figure this all out."

"Right." Only he wasn't so confident about that. He was worried about what was going to happen. He didn't want Adeline to get hurt.

He didn't want to ruin their friendship.

For the first time in a long time, he longed for what Aidan had. He wanted to be settled and that scared him.

It's only because Aidan and Shea are settled. You have something to prove.

But he shook the thought away.

It wasn't just that.

He wanted to stay with Adeline and his child. He wanted to settle down, but Adeline had made it clear that she didn't, and he didn't want to get his heart broken.

The thing was, his heart was already in danger.

He was falling for Adeline. Even though they had been in direct competition since he had landed in San Diego, he liked her.

She made life interesting.

There was so much he liked about her. She was smart, funny, sexy.

It was so easy to be with her.

He could be himself. His walls could be down. He didn't have to protect himself.

He loved working with her, and since their moment of passion, he couldn't get her out of his mind. He couldn't stop thinking about her in his arms. The taste of her kisses.

The way she had gotten under his skin. He wanted her.

He was falling for her and he was scared.

CHAPTER SEVEN

ELIAS WAS STILL trying to work out the crick in his neck from the previous night as he sat outside the hospital on his quick break. He thought he was drinking his seventeenth cup of coffee, but he couldn't quite be sure because he'd lost count. Either way, it was a lot of coffee.

He and Adeline had fallen asleep together on the couch. She had curled up with her head in his lap and he'd gone to sleep sitting up, so his head had fallen over the back of the couch and now he had a crick.

Which wasn't boding well for his long rotation at the hospital under the watchful eyes of the new doctors he had to impress.

And no matter how much coffee he drank, it wasn't helping.

He was just drained.

At least Adeline seemed to be doing better. The sickness that had plagued her yesterday didn't seem to be bothering her today as they made their rounds, checking on all the women who were admitted and taking new consultations on behalf of Dr. Wilder.

The baby of the first patient they saw was producing too much amniotic fluid and they would have to watch and drain the excess fluid. The baby was only twenty-eight weeks along, so the hope was that they could keep it in for longer.

The mother pregnant with twins had twin-to-twin transfusion syndrome, which was when one twin thrived and the other didn't. They were planning fetoscopic surgery to correct this syndrome, because Adeline already had experience doing a similar surgery successfully with Dr. Wilder.

Then there was a mother with gestational diabetes who had a high risk of complications, so they were going to be monitoring her.

The baby seemed to be fine, but Elias wasn't completely sure. Something about the pregnancy was not right. The mother was on bed rest, but Elias had a feeling that this baby would be making an appearance sooner rather than later.

"You look tired," Adeline said as she snuck up behind him.

"I am," he muttered, taking another sip of his coffee. "Next time we fall asleep together, can it be in a bed?"

"Noted. My shoulder is bothering me today." She sat down on the bench next to him. "We have another patient."

"Another patient?"

"Yes. She's gravida two para one. High-risk, not only because of her age, but because it's been a while since she's been pregnant, and her first baby was born early with heart issues and spent some time in the NICU. She wants to see a neonatologist."

"What does that have to do with me?" he asked, confused.

"Well, she heard a neonatologist from San Diego was working here and she demanded to see you. I examined her, and she's quite insistent. So I'm hoping you can come up with me and see her."

Elias's stomach twisted.

He had a bad feeling. *No. It couldn't be.*

"Take me to her." He crushed his coffee cup and tossed it in the garbage pail.

She wouldn't do this to me.

Only, he was pretty sure that she would. And as he followed Adeline back into the hospital to an exam room, he froze in his tracks when he saw a familiar fifteen-year-old boy sitting outside the exam room, focused on his phone.

Sure, he hadn't been home in two years, but he had kept in touch with his nephew.

Still, seeing him brought back a flood of emotions that he really wasn't prepared to deal with. Especially not in front of Adeline.

"Manny?" Elias asked.

Manny looked up and then smiled. "Uncle Elias!"

"Uncle?" Adeline asked.

Manny came and gave him a hug. At fifteen he was almost as tall as him and Elias was six foot two.

"What're you doing here?" Elias asked.

Manny nodded to the exam room. "Mom. She's pregnant again. We didn't think it would happen, but she is. There might be complications and she wants you there. She's a bit worked up. She was going to drive down to San Diego to see you."

Well, that explained why his sister had been getting so agitated the last few months when he had been ignoring her calls, texts, and emails.

"I've been busy, Manny. I'm sorry."

Manny nodded. "I get that, but Grandpa is sick too and Mom is hormonal. You haven't been home in a while, Uncle Elias."

"I know. Well, I had better go and see your mother before she starts tearing down the walls."

Manny laughed. "Good idea."

Elias sighed and Adeline followed him.

"So, she's your sister?" Adeline asked.

Elias nodded. "Yes. She's the oldest and the bossiest."

"She definitely knew what she wanted, but she didn't actually ask for Dr. Garcia. She just asked for that hotheaded, arrogant neonatologist from San Diego."

He paused and spun around to look at her. "And you instantly thought of me?"

Adeline grinned. "Who else? I had the same impression of you the first time I met you. Well, not the hotheaded part. The arrogant bit for sure."

"Arrogant?" he asked, playing offended.

"Oh, come on. You said something to me about not needing a babysitter the first time we met. Like I was some kind of glorified nanny."

He grinned. "So I did, but I wasn't the only arrogant one during that first meeting. She could mean you."

Adeline grinned. "I'm not as hotheaded and I'm not a neonatologist."

"Thanks." He opened the door. Adeline walked in first and then he followed.

Rosa spun around, her belly very large, and Elias had no doubt she would deliver soon. Thankfully, she hadn't dropped, so there was still time.

Her dark eyes landed on him and he knew that he was in trouble.

"Two years."

Elias sighed. "Dr. Turner, I'd like to introduce you to my sister, Rosa Adler."

"We've met," Adeline said, trying not to laugh.

"Two years," Rosa said again, ignoring the introduction.

"I've been learning how to become a surgeon,

Rosa! I was in Houston. I didn't have time to come home."

Rosa's eyes narrowed. "I suppose."

"And you want a consult with me?" Elias asked.

Rosa sat back down on the exam table. "I'm worried. I'm high-risk and it's been fifteen years since I had Manny."

Elias went to his sister's side. "I can't be your doctor. I'm your brother."

Rosa glanced at Adeline. "She can, right?"

"I can if you go into labor while I'm San Francisco. Don't you have a doctor in Napa?"

"I do, but I'm not happy with him." Rosa frowned. "The baby is large and there's a murmur in her heart. I'm scared. I heard you were here, and I don't fully trust those obstetricians in Napa."

Adeline stepped up. "Can I do an examination of you, Rosa?"

Rosa nodded.

"I'm going to walk outside and sit with Manny." Elias kissed his sister's head. "Try not to worry. Dr. Turner is one of the best."

Adeline smiled at him, her expression soft.

Elias left the room, walked down the hall and sat with Manny.

"How is your grandpa? The truth," Elias asked.

Manny frowned. "His heart. He needed a by-pass."

"Needed?" Elias asked.

"He had it, but he's still pretty weak."

"And what is Uncle Aidan doing?"

"Running the estate. He and Aunt Shea are having a baby in six months. I think."

Elias nodded. "So I heard."

No one had told him about Dad's bypass, but would that have changed anything?

His dad would still think the same of him.

It would've been nice to know what had happened, though.

To have been there for his dad.

But would you have taken the time off from work?

Elias wasn't sure and that thought upset him.

"It would be great to have you come home for a visit," Manny said, nudging him. "I miss you. Uncle Aidan is fine, but you're more fun!"

"Thanks, kid." Elias waited and soon Adeline opened the door. His sister came out of the room, moving slowly.

"Thank you, Dr. Turner. I really appreciate your help."

"My pleasure." Adeline headed back into the exam room to give them privacy. Which he appreciated.

"Elias, come home this weekend. Just for a

dinner or something. Do me this favor," Rosa begged.

Elias sighed. "Okay. I promise. I have time off Saturday and I'll come for dinner, okay?"

Rosa smiled and hugged him. "Great! Everyone will be so happy to see you."

Sure, they will.

"Take it easy." He hugged her again and watched as his sister and nephew walked down the hall.

He headed back into the exam room, where Adeline was cleaning up and making notes in her chart.

"How is she?"

"She's slightly dilated. I think you're going to have your niece before we leave. I am worried that her baby is measuring quite large and your sister had a C-section fifteen years ago, but everything else looks and sounds good. There's no reason to keep her in here."

Elias scrubbed his hand over his face. "I'm going to Napa to have dinner with my family. Do you want to come?"

Her eyes widened. "You want me to come?"

"In case she goes into labor. You said so yourself, she's dilated slightly."

"That's the only reason?"

Say yes.

"No." He couldn't. "My brother is married to my ex-fiancée. It would be nice if you came and pretended you were my fiancée. I mean, it's not that much of a stretch. We are having a baby together."

Adeline wasn't quite sure that she was hearing Elias correctly.

"You want me to...what?"

"Pretend to be my fiancée."

She was looking for some kind of sign that he was joking. He wasn't.

"Why do you want me to pretend to be your fiancée?"

"Remember about having something to prove?"

"I think you've had too much coffee." Although it might be kind of fun to pretend for a while.

What're you thinking? You turned him down flat not more than twenty-four hours ago.

Still, she felt bad that he had this issue with his family. That his parents viewed him as less than he was because he hadn't taken over the family estate. That his brother had married the woman he had been engaged to.

It seemed kind of messed up.

And she did want to check on Rosa Adler, Elias's sister. Adeline was worried about her. There was no medical reason to keep her admitted, but Adeline wanted to be close by in case Rosa went into labor. If Adeline were a betting person, she would lay serious money down on it happening this weekend.

"Okay." She couldn't believe she was agreeing to it.

Elias smiled. "Thank you. I owe you one."

"You bet you do," Adeline teased.

Her phone vibrated as did Elias's, and she frowned when she saw that it was the obstetrics team. It was about the baby of the mother who had high blood pressure. The patient's water had broken, and she was far enough along, but it was also time to deliver the twins.

"Ms. Saminsky. Her water broke and there's a lot of blood. You'd better get your NICU team ready. We're going to have to push back the twin-to-twin transfusion surgery."

Elias nodded. "Okay. I'll see you in the operating room."

Adeline nodded and made her way to the obstetrics inpatient floor, where there was a flurry of activity.

Dr. Wilder was on her way in from San Diego so that she could help with the twin-to-twin transfusion, but Adeline could handle a delivery of twins and a crash C-section if needed. She was an OB-GYN.

She grabbed a gown and headed into the room.

There was an undercurrent of panic and Adeline knew why. There was an awful lot of blood. Too much for a delivery. Something was wrong.

"We need to get her down to the OR now,"

Adeline said. "And I want the blood test ASAP. I need to know what is fetal and what is maternal."

As Adeline looked at the ultrasound, she could see that the placenta was lying low and she was sure that it was placenta previa. The placenta had grown on the cervix and torn away.

The patient had given no signs of going into preterm labor.

Still, all that mattered was getting her into the operating room and taking that baby out. Ms. Saminsky was rushed down the hall to the operating room, which was always prepped for cases such as this. The hospital in San Francisco was larger than San Diego Mesa Hospital.

It was a good system and Adeline was quite envious.

She was getting scrubbed up when Elias came into the scrub room.

"Placenta previa?" he asked.

Adeline nodded as she held up her arms and headed into the operating room. The patient was already out and the obstetrical staff had begun the C-section.

Adeline stepped in to assist.

The nurse who had run the blood sample to pathology came in. "Dr. Turner, it's maternal blood."

"Thank you!" Adeline was relieved. It meant that the umbilical cord hadn't torn away, but if it was maternal, then something else was going on.

As they worked to remove the baby, Adeline could see where the placenta had come away and ruptured some vessels.

She delivered the baby and handed it off to Elias and the NICU team.

She was worried about the baby, but right now, she had to repair the tear she found in the uterus, which was the reason for the maternal blood. The placenta previa had done the damage. As she focused on her work, she heard the tiny, quiet cry of the premature baby girl. And she smiled to herself, relieved to hear it.

She finished the repair on the mother.

"How is it going, Dr. Turner?"

Adeline looked up to see Dr. Wilder had come in.

"Placenta previa," Adeline responded.

Dr. Wilder nodded and remained on the periphery to watch. "Sorry to be the bearer of bad news, but you have only an hour before our next surgery. I have to fly back to San Diego tonight."

Adeline nodded. "I'll be ready, Dr. Wilder."

Adeline was exhausted and she was starving, but the twin-to-twin transfusion surgery had to happen today. Just like this one did.

"I can assist now, Dr. Wilder," Elias interjected.

Adeline glared at Elias, her heart sinking at him taking her surgery from her.

She thought they were friends. Why had she let her guard down?

You're in a competition, remember?

"Very good, Dr. Garcia. Come with me. Dr. Turner, come into the operating room when you're through."

Adeline nodded and focused on Ms. Saminsky.

And her job.

By the time Adeline finished the repair work on Ms. Saminsky, the twin-to-twin surgery was over. She was annoyed Elias had scooped it up, but she probably would have done the same thing if the situation were reversed.

She headed up to the NICU to see the twins.

She stood outside watching all the babies in the incubators. She could see Elias gowned and attending to the twins. She couldn't help but smile. He was so gentle and kind with those fragile twins.

How could anyone be disappointed in him?

Adeline felt uncomfortable going with Elias to meet his family, but her gut was telling her that it was the right thing to do. They were friends and she needed to support him.

Just like he was supporting her.

And Adeline liked Rosa.

So really this was for Rosa and for Elias.

Elias looked up and smiled at her. She waved back, her heart melting as she saw his hands were on a tiny baby, gently checking the vitals.

And all she could think about was their own baby. When she had found out she was pregnant yesterday, she hadn't allowed herself to think of the possibility of the future. The future, her pregnancy, it was all too real. For the first time in a long time she felt hope.

It made her feel happy and she had to smile.

Elias finished up his work and came out of the NICU to greet her.

"You look happy," he said.

"I feel happy."

Elias grinned at her. "I like to see you smiling. How is the mother?"

"She's stable. I'm just thankful you were able to deliver the twins. How are they doing?"

Elias glanced back. "They're strong. The smaller twin is slightly anemic, but we're taking care of that with platelets."

"Good. I'm just about to go over Ms. Saminsky's case with Dr. Wilder."

"Good luck."

She turned to leave, but then turned back.

"About this fake fiancée thing," she said. "What am I walking into?"

Elias sighed. "A lot of questions."

"We're not going to tell them about the baby yet. Right?"

She didn't want anyone knowing. Not yet. There were too many things that could go wrong.

"Right. That's our business." Elias sighed. "I appreciate you going along with this. And I mean it. I owe you one."

"Oh, what, a fellowship?" she teased. "Or a surgery?"

Elias laughed. "Go do your reporting and I'll see you later tonight. I'll make dinner."

"That sounds great."

Elias nodded and headed back into the NICU, and Adeline watched him as he continued on with his work.

She was so confused.

A month ago, she had had a purpose. She knew exactly where she was going with her life, but now, she didn't know what was happening. Her life was spiraling out of control and she couldn't even really think forward. Elias was making her feel things she hadn't felt in so long.

She didn't know what was going to happen.

And despite her optimism it frightened her.

She didn't want to get her hopes up.

About anything.

Elias finished in the NICU, and then he headed into the gallery of the operating room. There were residents, interns and some attendings watching Dr. Wilder and Adeline operating on an emergency uterine rupture that had come in.

It was an interesting operation and Elias didn't

often get a chance to watch Adeline work without being involved.

From the first time he had met her and done a surgery with her, Elias had been impressed with Adeline's ability, and seeing her with Dr. Wilder, it was apparent that she belonged here. That this was her calling.

"Dr. Garcia?"

Elias turned to see someone who could only be Dr. Spiner, the head of the NICU, standing beside him.

"Dr. Spiner?"

Dr. Spiner held out his hand and Elias shook it.

"I have to say that I have been very impressed with your and Dr. Turner's work here at the hospital."

"Thank you."

Dr. Spiner took a deep breath. "I don't like trying to poach a surgeon from another, but if you're ever looking for a position, I would gladly have you as an attending here at our hospital."

If it had been a couple of months ago, Elias might have taken Dr. Spiner up on his offer, but would he have stuck with it?

Probably not.

He was still focused on the fellowship. Dr. Wilder was in San Diego.

And so was Adeline.

So was his baby.

He couldn't leave them.

"Thank you for the offer, Dr. Spiner. I will keep it in mind, but…"

"But what?" Dr. Spiner asked.

"Dr. Turner and I are expecting." He winced, because he had let it slip. That's not what he'd wanted to do. "It's quite early. We haven't told anyone."

"Well, we would love to have Dr. Turner on board too." Dr. Spiner smiled. "She's a fine surgeon and I was going to ask her first if I'm honest. She'd make an excellent OB/GYN Attending here. I would love to have her."

Elias held up his hand. "She wants to stay with Dr. Wilder. So do I."

Dr. Spiner nodded. "I understand. Well, if you two ever change your mind, San Francisco is a great place to raise a family."

"Thank you, Dr. Spiner."

Elias rubbed his temples as Dr. Spiner walked away.

What did you just do?

The one thing that Adeline had asked him not to do was tell anyone about her pregnancy, not until after the fellowship had been decided, and he'd done the exact opposite.

He'd let it slip.

He just had to hope that Adeline didn't find out, that no one said anything to her, because he'd broken her trust.

And he knew that trust was very important to

Adeline. He was angry with himself. He might have just ruined everything.

And the thought scared him.

The thought that he might lose it all.

CHAPTER EIGHT

ADELINE DIDN'T GET back to the apartment until early in the morning. Back-to-back surgeries had wreaked havoc on her.

She was glad to do a one-on-one surgery with Dr. Wilder. Especially after Elias had poached the twin-to-twin surgery.

Still, everywhere ached.

And then Dr. Wilder had stuck around a bit longer to check on the progress of the twin-to-twin transfusion surgery, which had been done by endoscopic laser ablation. And then there had been charting and reports.

Then she had seen Dr. Wilder off to the airport before heading back to the apartment.

Elias was in bed when she got back, but in the fridge was a small plate of pasta and a salad that he'd left for her.

It was so thoughtful, tears stung her eyes.

What're you doing? Why are you crying over spaghetti?

No one had ever done something like this for her before.

Except her mom.

Ever since she'd been hurt by Gregory, she'd relied on herself.

She never let herself down.

But this dinner left for her, it was so sweet.

Adeline brushed the tears away. These hormones drove her bonkers.

This was getting ridiculous. This was not like her, but then again, she had never been pregnant before either.

It was a whole new scope of stuff to think about. She remembered how, long before she went to medical school, she had been this vulnerable, happy, full of hope.

She'd been focused on her goals, but they hadn't completely defined her.

When Gregory had betrayed her trust and broken her heart, it had nearly ruined everything. At that moment, all she had been able to think about was how she'd let her mother down, because for one brief moment back then she had thought it would be easier to step away from her career.

She had been so ashamed at what had happened, she had wanted to give up medicine.

Which would have meant giving up on finding a cure for TTP.

It would have meant giving up on her mother.

But then she had come to her senses, girded her loins and gone back to school.

She never had told her parents what had actually happened when she had taken that small leave from medical school and then switched schools.

It still ate away at her all these years later, but that was her problem. Not her mother's. Everything Adeline had ever done in her career was for her mother, as it was Adeline's pregnancy that had caused that recessive gene in her mother to kick in.

Adeline heated up her food and then wandered over to the little table and chairs by the window. The park was dark, but that didn't bother her. There was a window open in the apartment and she could hear the wind whispering through the trees.

It was calming.

There had been a lot of times when she was a teenager that she had come to either the Panhandle or the larger Golden Gate Park, which the Panhandle attached to, and she had listened to the trees.

That was something she missed in San Diego, but she did like being close to the water.

Her phone buzzed with a text message. It was from her mom.

Saw you on the news. Big surgery. Didn't know you were here. Call when you get a chance. Love you.

Adeline hit the speed dial for her mother.

"Hi, Mom," she said.

"I thought you might still be awake," her mother said brightly.

"What're you doing up this late?" Adeline asked.

"Couldn't sleep. I had a flare-up earlier this week, so I've been on TPE again."

Adeline's throat constricted. "You haven't had a flare-up in so long."

"I know. I guess I was due." Her mother sighed. "I'm okay, but I thought I would remind you about genetic testing. I know that you said you never wanted to get it done…"

"I got it done, Mom," Adeline said gently.

"You did?" There was both relief and worry in her voice.

"Still don't have the results, but I did get it done."

"I'm so glad you did. What made you change your mind? You were so dead against it."

"My…" Adeline hesitated. She didn't want to tell her mother about the pregnancy, especially when she didn't know the outcome of the ge-netic testing. And she certainly didn't want her mother to think that there was something going on with Elias.

Mom had been one of the people pushing her to move and try again since Gregory. She may not have told her mom the whole story about Gregory, only that she saw someone and when the relationship ended it broke her heart. That's all her mother needed to know. Adeline didn't want to get her hopes up.

"My?" her mother asked.

"One of my roommates in San Diego made me see sense, you know? I may not want a family, but what if it is genetic and just hits one day? It would be good for my doctors to know."

"Exactly," her mother said, but Adeline could hear that disappointment in her voice. The disappointment her mother always had when Adeline talked about not wanting a family.

It stung her to lie to her mom.

It stung her to lie to herself.

"I'm so glad you got the test done, Adeline."

"I am too. I hate the waiting, even though I know genetic testing can take time."

Her mother laughed. "Doctors can be so patient and impatient at the same time."

"I know." Adeline smiled.

"So, when are you coming to see me?"

"I'm busy this weekend. We're here for a couple of weeks, so I hope that I can come and see you next week one night. I can come over for dinner."

"Where are you staying? Are you in a hotel? Because if you are, I'm sending your father over there now. There's no sense in you being in a hotel."

Adeline chuckled. "I'm not in a hotel, Mom. There's an apartment across from the Panhandle. The hospital owns it and it's close by."

Her mother sighed. "You're right, that's better. But I do hope you come and see me soon."

"I will, Mom. I promise."

"Night, Adeline."

"Night, Mom."

Adeline hung up the phone and then looked up to see Elias standing in the kitchen.

"Sorry, did I wake you?"

"No. I was only dozing. I was half listening for you," he said. He still sounded tired.

"Dude, you weren't dozing when I went to check on you. You were flat on your back snoring." Which was true. It was kind of cute.

"I don't snore," he said with indignation.

"You so do," Adeline teased.

"I'm insulted. I make you a nice dinner, and you don't come home until late and accuse me of snoring."

"You sound like an unhappy spouse."

Elias chuckled. "I suppose I do. How was the surgery?"

Adeline sighed. "Long. It was long, and I'm beat."

"Well, you need to forget about cleaning those dishes and get to bed, because you're going to need your strength dealing with my family tomorrow."

"Okay. That sounds kind of ominous."

Elias nodded and headed back down the hall to his bedroom.

Adeline finished her dinner, which had gotten cold again after talking to her mother.

It was so easy to fall into a routine with Elias. It was so easy to talk to him. He got through her barriers. He took care of her.

He cared about her.

Or it seemed that way. She was worried about her heart, her baby.

It was one thing to put her heart on the line, but she had her baby to think about.

She had to protect her child from being hurt.

Her rules protected her from heartache, but when it came to Elias, she was doing a horrible job of disobeying the rules she had set for herself since Gregory broke her heart.

Was it her adaptability that was trying to hijack her consistent life?

Either way, she had to regain control, but Adeline knew that was trying to hold on to sand in the water. It was just slipping away.

* * *

Elias was tense when he rented a car. He had been dreading this drive, but Adeline seemed in good spirits, so thankfully Dr. Spiner hadn't let it slip that he knew Adeline was pregnant.

"I wish you had rented a convertible," Adeline teased as Elias pulled up in an SUV.

"They didn't have any and it's really windy today. Why would you want a convertible?" he asked, puzzled.

"I don't know. I've always wanted to take a trip in one."

He smiled. "You need to rent a convertible to go down the coast, not up it."

"Who says?" she asked, tossing her overnight bag into the back.

He eyed the bag with misgivings. "Why did you pack a bag?"

"I have a feeling we won't be leaving tonight."

"What gives you that idea? Napa is only an hour away."

"Your sister is due and I think that she will likely give birth in the next forty-eight hours."

Elias's eyes widened. "Shouldn't we get her admitted?"

"There's no medical reason to admit her, but since we're off the next two days, I thought it would be wise to bring an overnight bag on the off chance. I know for a fact that Napa has a hospital and I can get privileges there. That's if she still wants me to be her doctor."

"Okay. I'll be back."

He was going with Adeline's gut instinct on this, as so far her instincts had never been wrong.

Except for when she thought that she had a cold and was actually pregnant.

Adeline had even thought it was absurd at first.

He knew she didn't want a family, that she was scared of the genetic condition, but she seemed almost at peace with it all now and Elias couldn't help but wonder if there was more. She was holding something back, but he didn't know what.

Something that scared her.

He didn't know much about her previous relationship.

Only that it had almost cost her her career.

What happened?

He wanted to know more, but he was so afraid of pushing her away. He hated feeling this uncertainty. He was already on edge at the thought of going to see his family. At the thought he might run into Aidan.

This is what his family did to him and he hadn't even left San Francisco yet. He quickly packed an overnight bag and locked up.

Adeline was leaning against the side of the SUV, and she looked so cute in her oversized cardigan and big sunglasses. He loved it when her hair was down and loose. He could remember how soft and luxurious it felt when they had made love.

"You ready?" she asked, smiling. She seemed so at ease in San Francisco. As if she was at peace here, and he couldn't blame her.

He'd forgotten how much he loved this city too. It had been too long since he'd been back.

And he heard his father's voice in his head.

Always wandering. You need to put down roots. Settle down.

He couldn't come back to San Francisco until he had the fellowship.

There were fine doctors here and he would be proud to be counted among them, but he wasn't going to abandon his child or the fellowship. He'd worked too hard.

Even though he had never really wanted to be trapped by marriage, he was sort of trapped. Wherever Adeline went, he would go, because wherever she went, that's where his child would be. The feeling of anxiety rose up in him again, like a heavy weight hovering over him, threatening to drop on him at any moment.

He glanced at Adeline and that heavy feeling dissipated.

Being near Adeline calmed him as well as terrified him.

"You okay?" she asked, frowning. "You look a bit introspective."

"Just preparing for this car ride up to my family's place." Which wasn't a total lie. He wasn't exactly excited about driving up to Napa either, but he didn't want to tell Adeline what he was actually worried about.

Losing her.

Losing his child.

"It'll be okay. It may be windy, but it's a sunny day!"

"When did you become so positive?" Elias teased as he opened the door for her.

"I can blame that on pregnancy." She winked.

"Perhaps. You're usually so uptight and serious. Now you seem carefree. I like it."

"See, I guess the hormones are helping me relax."

"Well, I should get you pregnant more often."

"Ha ha," she said dryly.

Elias chuckled and then walked around to the other side of the car and opened the door. "So, what you're really saying is that I'm responsible for your happiness now, rather than your anger or wrath or whatever else you thought of me when we first met."

"I suppose so."

"Well, then I'll take that as a compliment." He pulled out of the parking spot and they headed down through the hilly streets of San Francisco, making their way to the Golden Gate Bridge. It would be a beautiful drive, but it was also busy, as everyone seemed to have the same idea on

Saturday to drive out of the city and head north up the coast.

The hour-long ride was taking a bit longer than he thought, so that by the time they got to Silverado Springs, they had already been in the car for two hours and it was lunchtime. He found a small bistro just off the main route and parked out front.

"What're we doing here?" Adeline asked.

"Getting you something to eat. We've been in the car two hours and we're only in Silverado Springs. We should be to my parents' place by now. I think we need a break."

She nodded. "Text your sister and tell her why we're late. I have a feeling she's a worrier."

Elias snorted. "You don't know the half of it."

And when he pulled out his phone, he could see there were already several texts from his sister, wondering where he was.

He texted her back that they were stuck in traffic and taking a quick break in Silverado Springs and that they would be there in about forty minutes or so.

They found a little table outside and ordered a light lunch.

Elias had a hard time holding on to any thread of a conversation, because he was thinking about what was waiting for him at his family's estate.

It had been two years, as his sister liked to remind him, since he had been home.

And even before that, once he had started college, his visits home had been sporadic at best. His father and he had never seen eye to eye. His father saw duty, family, and family history, also known as the vineyard, as the most important things.

Elias valued his education.

He and his dad saw things very differently.

But maybe not that differently. His father valued the land and Elias valued education and medicine. Both of them worked hard.

Perhaps Elias had been too tough on him.

He's always been tough on you.

Still, there was a part of Elias that wished things were different and he hadn't spent so many years rejecting the vineyard, rejecting everything his father offered.

He hated himself a bit for that.

His stomach sank and dread crept down his spine.

He was not looking forward to any part of this reunion.

"You're looking pensive again," Adeline said.

"I feel pensive." Elias scrubbed a hand over his face.

"Tell me what I'm getting into. You've told me a bit but…"

"My dad and I don't really talk. My brother married my ex-fiancée. Do I need to go on?"

A strange look crossed her face, but it was a

brief flicker, almost as if she was jealous. He didn't intend it to be that way.

"That's going to be hard," she finally said, but she wasn't looking at him. Instead she was pushing a radish around with her fork on her plate.

Elias reached out and took her hand. "Hey, I'm over her. I'm over Shea."

Adeline's cheeks flushed pink and she took back her hand. "Okay. I'm glad to hear that."

An awkward silence fell between them.

He hated the way that the subject of Shea had caused this tension between them.

That the easiness between them had gone.

He missed it.

He had thought for a moment that Adeline might be jealous, thinking that he was still in love with Shea. He wanted to reassure her. He wasn't in love with Shea anymore. They had drifted apart. He had put medical school first.

Why her? Elias had shouted.

I love her, Aidan had snapped. *You were never there for her. I was there when you weren't. Face it: school is so important to you, you even threw away the woman you loved.*

How dare you?

You only care about yourself, Elias. You don't see other people.

That thought sobered him. Perhaps Adeline didn't care, or didn't care romantically, at least. And he was only seeing what he wanted to see.

She doesn't want a relationship with you.

He had to keep telling himself that. Adeline had made it perfectly clear that she didn't want them to be a couple. That their relationship was just platonic, except for the one time that had resulted in their baby.

"Well, we'd better get going or my sister will be texting again," he teased, trying to brush off the awkward silence.

"Sounds good. I'm kind of hoping she'll let me examine her. I'm concerned that she'll go into labor soon."

"I think she will. She's not a fool. Any chance to have her own private doctor for the weekend."

They split the bill and headed back to the car, neither of them saying anything. Not that there was much to say after that awkward moment.

He didn't love Shea anymore. She had made her choice. And as far as Elias was concerned, she and Aidan deserved each other. Nothing had changed, and he wasn't going to open his heart to anyone.

Only, the inner monologue he was telling himself over and over again wasn't cutting it anymore. As he looked at Adeline, he was hoping for more of a reaction. He wanted to see that she cared for him. That he wasn't making it up in his head.

That she needed him as much as he needed her. He wanted her to care, because even though he hated to admit it, even though he couldn't face it, his heart was telling him that he was losing a battle.

And that he was falling for Adeline.

The problem was, he knew that it was going to end with his heart broken.

CHAPTER NINE

SOMETHING HAD CHANGED at that bistro and Adeline knew without a shadow of a doubt that it was her. When Elias had talked about his ex—the woman who had broken his heart—she had had a momentary flash of jealousy.

Even though she didn't want anything from him.

Or she had gone into this whole thing saying that she didn't want anything, but now...now she didn't know what she wanted. She was confused.

She tried to brush it off, tried to act like she didn't care, but that seemed to make it worse and she was angry with herself for that.

The closer they got to his family's estate, the more she could see he was visibly tensing. This was going to be a long day or two and now she was regretting agreeing to come.

"Do you want me to drive? You look like you're about to snap that steering wheel in half," she teased, hoping that it would break some of the tension.

He smiled and relaxed a little. "Sorry. They just…it's been a while, and my father is a bit stubborn."

"It'll be okay."

"Don't be so certain." He sighed. "Although he might be more mellow with you around. He was always a sucker for a pretty face."

She blushed. "It'll just be the moments the two of you are alone, then."

"That's doubtful. Aidan has never let Dad and me talk alone since he took over the estate. It's like he thinks that I'm coming to take it back…" He trailed off and cleared his throat. "I have no desire to ever take over the vineyard. Wine is not my passion."

"Medicine is. I get that."

"You never told me what your family does."

"My dad works in IT and my mother was a teacher. Not really a family business you can take over. Although my brother, Kyle, did become an IT guy too."

"And you went into medicine?"

She nodded. "I've always wanted to save the most fragile lives. Dr. Wilder can help me with that."

"You have to stop putting Dr. Wilder on a pedestal," he said quickly.

"What do you mean?" she asked.

"You're just as talented as Dr. Wilder. You're a

good surgeon. You've been studying and learning your specialty for a long time. You've been so focused on this course."

"I'm not as good as Dr. Wilder," she muttered.

"Dr. Spiner thinks you are. He thinks highly of you."

Her eyes widened. She was completely shocked. "What're you talking about?"

"Dr. Spiner offered me a job and said that he would be more than happy to take us both on as attendings."

She was floored. Adeline hadn't been offered many positions before, not that she had gone out seeking one either. The only goal she had had since her days as an undergraduate was to work with Dr. Wilder. She had wanted to learn.

Everything.

"You seemed surprised."

"I am," she whispered.

"Don't be. You're talented, Adeline, and you deserve job offers."

"Well, he hasn't actually offered me a job yet."

"And when he does?" Elias asked. "I know he will."

"Well, no. I want a fellowship with Dr. Wilder. That's been my goal since I started medical school."

"Because she's one of the best?"

"Yes. She wrote a paper on TTP and it was

brilliant. Everything I've been working toward has been about that and I'm so close."

"Well, I just wanted you to know that you have options, Adeline. You're more talented than you give yourself credit for. You handled that first surgery, that vasa previa, with expertise, and those babies are alive because of you. And I was watching your surgery on the uterine rupture. It was you who was leading. It wasn't Dr. Wilder."

They turned off the main road and then headed down a gravel road that was lined with trees, but she couldn't focus on the beautiful scenery. All she could think about was that he was watching her and his encouraging words.

She wanted to believe what he was saying was true, but that self-doubt part of her was telling her that he was lying. Elias was just telling her these things because he wanted her to drop out of the competition. She shook that thought away. Elias might have been her competition once, but now they were friends.

She trusted him.

He hadn't accepted Dr. Spiner's offer either.

Was he trying to push her to accept so that he could obtain the fellowship position?

That's not it.

Elias wasn't like that. Elias was not Gregory. He cared for her. He'd been a friend and looked out for her.

Elias made her feel safe.

Elias made her think that anything could happen.

Only, she was having a hard time reconciling that with her fears. She was having a hard time daring to dream. She was having a hard time trusting her gut instinct, which upset her greatly.

Her gut instinct was something she relied on, and she was so angry that her thoughts were all scrambled and she couldn't think straight.

It's pregnancy hormones.

That seemed to rationalize it all in her head. If she weren't pregnant, then she wouldn't be so confused.

Elias slowed the SUV as they approached a stone gate. It had an ironwork sign overhead that stated they were entering Garcia Estates Winery.

"We're here," Elias said through clenched teeth.

"Hey, it'll be okay." Although now she was feeling a bit worried too. She was here on a ruse. She was here pretending to be Elias's fiancée. She didn't usually like deceiving people. She didn't like lying.

They drove down the tree-lined road, which eventually opened up to a beautiful valley where there were rows and rows of vines over the rolling hills of green. To the west were foothills that led to the Mayacama Mountain Range of the Northern Inner Coast Mountains.

It was absolutely stunning.

"Elias, it's beautiful here," she gasped.

"Yes. It is, but it's hard work. My father won't let you forget that," he teased.

They continued on their drive toward the large, sprawling ranch house that had a Spanish influence with its red tiled roof and whitewashed clay walls.

The main drive in front of the house was made of terra-cotta stones, and large box elder trees blew in the wind.

"We're here." Elias was still gripping the wheel. "Are you sure you're okay with this?"

"What? Pretending to be your fiancée…no, but I'll be okay. That's what friends are for." And she tried to smile encouragingly at him.

"Right." Only he didn't look so encouraged. His lips were pressed together in a thin line. That sparkle, that twinkle of mischievousness that was usually in his eyes, was gone.

This was serious Elias.

He parked the SUV and got out to open the door for her.

"Well, at least I did teach you some manners," a deep voice boomed out.

Adeline spun around to see a big tall man who was about sixty-five, maybe older, given the worn leather look to his skin, which she attributed to his working outside probably most of his life. His eyes were the same as Elias's, though, and his jawline.

He was a very handsome man.

"Dad," Elias said tightly. "May I introduce you to my fiancée, Dr. Adeline Turner."

The old man's piercing gaze fell on her and she tried to keep calm and collected.

Elias's pulse was thundering in his ears as he stared at his father.

He slipped his arm around Adeline, who was trying very hard to go along with it all. She had an extra-wide smile on her face, grinning a little bit too much as Elias held her.

"Fiancée?" his father asked, cocking one of his silver eyebrows.

"Yes." Elias nodded. "Dr. Turner is an OB-GYN and she, like me, is training under Dr. Wilder in San Diego."

"Yes. Rosa told us you had moved back to California from Texas." His father turned his gaze to Adeline. Instantly the hard expression that had been focused on Elias softened, and he smiled.

"Welcome to our home, Adeline. I'm Jimeno Garcia. It's my pleasure to meet you."

"Same," Adeline said, taking his hand.

His father held her hand. "I don't see a ring?"

"That's because it's fairly new—the engagement—and we haven't picked it out yet. Also, it's hard for me to wear rings in my line of work. I'm always in and out of the operating room."

His dad's eyes tracked between Elias and Adeline. "Well, we're glad you're here. Your mother is waiting for you in the kitchen. I have to meet Aidan in the fields. Some of the vines are sick, but I know that's not the kind of doctoring you two do."

And without further words, his father ambled off towards the hill at the side of the house to make his way down to the barns.

Elias was fuming.

No *welcome home, son*. Nothing.

At least he was kind to Adeline.

Adeline hit him in the arm. "You had me so worried. He was nice."

"I'm sorry. Ow! Don't hit me." He rubbed his arm. "Besides, he is nice to strangers and beautiful women."

Adeline sighed and then smiled. "Well, just make sure you don't actually tell them the truth of our situation."

"They're eventually going to know."

"I know." Adeline rubbed her temples. "I know."

"Come on, let's go see my mom before my dad comes back and chastises me for lingering too long in the driveway or something."

Adeline chuckled.

He opened the front door and kicked off his shoes. Adeline kicked off her sandals, and he led her through the open concept house that he knew so well and headed to the large kitchen at the back. It had floor-to-ceiling windows and a large deck that overlooked the vineyard.

"Mom," Elias said.

His mother was a small woman, with the same dark curly hair as Elias and his sister, Rosa. Her eyes widened and she smiled, her arms open.

"Elias! Finally, you're home!" She embraced her son and then hit him in the arm. "Two years, and you have been back in California for a few months, I hear, and yet you haven't come to see me."

"San Diego is not an hour away," Elias said. "And I'm a surgeon. I've been busy."

His mother's gaze turned to Adeline and she smiled politely. "Hello?"

"This is my fiancée, Dr. Adeline Turner."

His mother's eyes widened further. "Fiancée?"

"It's lovely to meet you, Mrs. Garcia." Adeline took the woman's hand in hers.

"Call me Flora. And it's lovely to meet you too. You're a doctor as well?" Flora asked.

"I am. I'm an OB-GYN and I'm specializing in maternal-fetal surgery."

Flora smiled. "No wonder you two are together. You're both interested in the same thing. That makes sense and it explains why you haven't been home, but where's the ring?"

"It's a new engagement, Mom. We haven't had

a chance to pick one out yet. We will," he said quickly, opting for the same excuse that Adeline had given his dad.

Flora nodded, her eyes still wide, and Elias knew that he had completely shocked his mother.

"Well, I'm so happy." Flora smiled again. "Welcome to the family, Adeline. Now I can show you upstairs to your room so you can freshen up."

"Mom, how did you know we were going to stay?"

Flora laughed. "I was going to make sure of it. Some nice wine…a lot of food. You'd have no choice."

Elias rolled his eyes but laughed as his mother cleaned her hands and then led them out of the kitchen, up the stairs, and down a long hall. She opened the door to the big guest room at the end.

"You two should be comfortable here. Are your bags in the car? Shall I send Manny to get them?"

"No, Mom. We'll get them in a bit. We'll freshen up and we'll come back down."

Flora nodded and then kissed him on the cheek. "So glad you're home."

Elias shut the door as she left.

"Your mother is going to wonder why I can't drink wine tonight," Adeline stated.

"We'll tell her you're on call. That will do it." He shrugged out of his leather jacket and set it on the bed.

"So, we're supposed to spend the night here. Together?"

"We are engaged," he said.

"No, we're not!" she hissed.

"We've been together before, Adeline. It won't be that bad."

Her pulse thundered in her ears and all she could see was that bed.

An image of him kissing her neck flashed through her mind.

It fired her blood with the promised pleasure she knew could be found in his arms.

Get a hold of yourself.

She needed to change the subject fast.

Her eyes narrowed, but she was smiling beneath that frown. "You keep your pants on, mister. I know you sleep naked."

"And how do you know that?" he asked, smiling.

She blushed. "I just do."

He grinned lazily. "No promises."

Adeline sat on the bed. "So, are you going out to the SUV to get the bags?"

"Why the rush?" he asked.

"I'm tired. I'm hoping I can take a nap, trying to get over this nausea if I'm going to play fiancée tonight."

"Okay. I'll go get the bags. You put your feet up. You're going to need the rest."

Elias left the room and shut the door. He made his way down the hall and slipped on his shoes, then went straight to the SUV and pulled the two bags out of the back.

"I didn't know that you were planning to stay the weekend."

The voice made him freeze, made his heart skip a beat, but this time in fear. Other times that voice had been like the voice of an angel. It had made his heart skip a beat in happiness, but now it was just a reminder of past pain. How they had grown apart.

Now it didn't mean anything to him.

It just made him numb.

He turned around to see Shea standing there. It was like nothing had changed. Still that gorgeous brown hair, olive skin, lithe figure. Except now there was a visible bump that reminded him of what he had always hoped for.

Only it was his brother's baby.

Not his. And he didn't care because Adeline was pregnant with his baby.

And he smiled, thinking of Adeline and his child.

Seeing Shea wasn't as painful as he'd thought it would be.

"We weren't sure, but Mom insisted." He didn't say any more, and he looked at her, remembering when she had left him.

We've grown apart, Elias. You've been at school and Aidan's been here for me. When my parents died, you didn't come home because you had exams. Aidan was there. I love him.

You don't love me?

I do, but I love Aidan more. He was here for me. You never were. I'm sorry it has to be this way, Elias. I'm sorry.

She'd handed back the ring, placing it in his palm.

You have big dreams, but I don't have those dreams. I belong here.

That memory had haunted him, but now it didn't matter.

It didn't hurt as much.

"We?" Shea asked, intrigued.

"My fiancée. Dr. Adeline Turner, one of the best OB-GYNs on the West Coast."

Shea cocked an eyebrow. "I think I read about her in the newspaper. She saved a baby and is taking consults with Dr. Wilder."

"Yes. I was there during it. She saved the mother. I saved the baby."

Shea smiled sweetly. "I look forward to meeting her."

Elias nodded quickly. He needed to put some space between him and Shea. He didn't want to be around her, but surprisingly, it wasn't as bad as he had pictured it. It didn't sting as much as he had thought it would.

That's because of Adeline and your baby.

Even if Adeline didn't want him, he wanted her.

And his parents seemed to like Adeline.

Certainly more than they had liked Shea at first.

He knew his parents hadn't been happy with Aidan and Shea, but two years ago they had made amends when Aidan took over the bulk of the vineyard work, and that's when Elias had stopped coming home.

"Well, I'm going to bring her her bag. She's a bit tired. Double surgeries yesterday and the traffic on the bridge was terrible. That's why we were so delayed."

Shea nodded. "Okay. I'll see you both at dinner."

Elias turned back to the house.

He was hoping that Shea and Aidan would stay at their own house on the other side of the property, but by the sound of his mother's plan, she was going to have the whole family for dinner.

Like a reunion.

And he was in no mood for a reunion after having run into both his father and Shea.

Now all that was left was running into Aidan again.

And Elias knew that he would need a few

glasses of wine before he had the patience and the strength to stand up to his brother.

The man who had to have everything he did.

Well, he couldn't have Adeline.

And he knew then that Adeline was all that mattered. For one brief second, he wished that their ruse wasn't fake.

He wished that they were actually engaged.

That she was really his. But he knew how she felt. And Elias wasn't about to put his heart at risk again.

He couldn't stand another dream being taken away, because the dream he wanted more than anything to come true was him, Adeline and the baby.

Together.

Forever.

But he knew that wasn't possible. That wasn't going to happen. One of them would get the fellowship. One of them had to walk away from it, and the sooner he got over that silly flight of fancy, the better.

Though he wasn't sure he could.

CHAPTER TEN

ADELINE WOKE WITH a start, not realizing she'd dozed off. The sun was lower in the sky and Elias was nowhere to be found, but the bags were in the room. She checked her phone and she'd only been asleep an hour. She rose and cleaned herself up before venturing out.

When she stepped into the hall, she ran smack-bang into Rosa.

"Dr. Turner." Rosa crossed her arms. "The least you could've done was told me you were engaged to my brother!"

"Are you always this confrontational?" Adeline asked.

Rosa smirked. "Yes."

"Well, we weren't engaged at the time I met you, and if you remember, that day was quite hectic."

"Fine." Rosa relaxed and then smiled brightly. "I am glad he's moved on."

Adeline eyed Rosa very carefully. Her belly

had been high the day they met, but now it was low. Quite low.

"Your baby has dropped," Adeline remarked. "Have you contacted the hospital in Napa?"

Rosa nodded. "Last night. My husband is out of town on business and I was contemplating heading back to San Francisco with you and Elias, but I hear that you're staying here for now. So I'll stick close to you if I can?"

"I am, or rather we are." Adeline frowned. "Rosa, can I check you? You're moving awfully slowly."

"Sure. The room I'm staying in is just over here."

"Okay. I'll grab my bag and I'll meet you over there." Adeline was really thankful that she had brought a medical kit with her. She just knew that Rosa was going to be close to delivery. And she was not surprised to find out that the baby had dropped. At the last exam, Rosa had been fifty percent effaced and dilated one centimeter.

She headed across the hall and knocked on the door.

"Come in," Rosa called out.

Adeline headed in there and Rosa was on the bed. Adeline pulled out her stethoscope and listened to the baby. The baby's heartbeat was strong. She felt where the baby was sitting.

"She's engaged and head-down. That's a good

AMY RUTTAN

sign. She is measuring quite large. Did your OB in Napa say anything about a large baby?"

"No. Well, other than telling me I couldn't have a VBAC and scheduling my C-section, but this OB is pro always doing a C-section. I'm glad she's head-down."

"What happened with your son, Manny, when you had him?" Adeline asked.

"He was born early at thirty weeks. It was a C-section. And he had patent ductus arteriosus, a hole in his heart. It was quite large and was closed when he was four. He spent a lot of time in the NICU. Ultrasounds showed that my daughter has a PDA as well. I'm worried."

"I can't check for sure without an ultrasound or a Doppler, but what I'm hearing sounds good. Nothing in distress. How are you feeling?"

"Tired. Sore. Ready for it to be over."

"I'm sure you are." Adeline held out her hands to help Rosa sit up. "Do you want my professional opinion?"

"My future sister-in-law's professional opinion?" Rosa grinned.

That stunned Adeline for a moment. And it stunned her because she didn't the find the idea horribly wrong. In fact, she didn't mind it at all. The thought of being Elias's wife gave her a thrill of pleasure.

It had shocked her when Elias had first suggested she pretend to be his fiancée, but she liked

Rosa. She liked all the Garcia family members she'd met, although she was worried about meeting the woman who had held Elias's heart before.

And she couldn't help but wonder if this woman had the same hold on Elias still, because Elias had been worried about coming home.

He hadn't been home in two years because his brother married his ex.

Was he still in love with her? Is that what he was hiding and why he was acting so strangely? There was another part of her that was a bit jealous.

Even though she didn't want to open her heart to anyone again, she was jealous of the woman who came before her because she had something that Adeline would never have.

Elias's heart. It made her sad. It made her envious.

"Yes," Adeline said, shaking that thought away. "Yes, on the professional advice of your future sister-in-law."

"What is it?" Rosa asked.

"I think you need to call your husband home. I think this baby will be coming in the next couple of days and I hope you have your go bag ready for a trip to the Napa hospital."

Rosa looked terrified. "Oh, okay."

"I'll be here this weekend. Your brother wanted to return to San Francisco, but I think I'll be able to convince him to stay." Adeline smiled. "Don't worry. Everything will be okay."

Rosa nodded. "Thank you, Dr.… .thank you, Adeline."

"No problem. Now, do you think you could tell me where Elias has wandered off to?" Adeline asked, packing up her gear.

"I think he was out on the deck, watching the sunset. Since Aidan is in the field…" Rosa trailed off. "How much has Elias told you?"

"A bit," Adeline said. "Aidan is married to the woman Elias was first engaged to."

Rosa worried her bottom lip. "Yes. Elias was in love with Shea, but… I'm not sure she was fully committed to Elias. It was a strange relationship and they grew apart. He rarely came home, and Shea hardly saw him. Aidan was here and… It was hard. My parents weren't exactly thrilled with how everything turned out, but Shea and Aidan are happy and now that Elias has found you, everything has worked out!"

Adeline nodded. "Right."

Elias hadn't found her.

They didn't have a relationship. Sure, she was having his baby, but that was it. There was no relationship. There was no family rift being repaired, but she had promised Elias that she would keep up this pretense.

That's what friends were for.

And that's all she and Elias were.

Friends. And soon that would be over, when one of them got the fellowship and the other walked away. Except she wanted more. She wanted to be his. She wanted to have his heart.

And she wanted to give him hers, but she was too scared to.

"I'll see you at dinner tonight," Adeline said. "I'd better go find Elias."

"I'll see you tonight." Rosa smiled.

Adeline left Rosa's room and headed back across the hall to the guest suite. She set her case on the bed and walked out through the balcony doors onto the large deck. She found him sitting on a deck chair, his eyes closed.

"Relaxed?" Adeline asked.

"Not really," Elias murmured. "How was your nap?"

"Good. I ran into your sister, Rosa."

Elias sat up straighter. "How is she?"

"The baby has dropped."

Elias's eyes widened. "Really? So then your hunch was right."

"Seems to be on that track."

"So, are you suggesting we stick around?"

Adeline nodded. "Yes. The baby may have the same PDA as your nephew, Manny, and given the large size she's measuring, I'm worried about her being so far from a hospital. How far is it to the Napa hospital?"

"Thirty minutes," Elias stated.

"And if there is any issue, that's too long." Adeline chewed on her bottom lip. "Look, I know you're uncomfortable with your family, but when we return to San Francisco, if Rosa hasn't delivered, she needs to come back to the city with us."

Elias nodded. "Agreed. I really didn't want to stay long, but... I have nothing against Rosa. I don't have a problem with her, and I've missed her."

"It's just your brother and your dad."

Elisa nodded. "I ran into my ex. She's pregnant."

"How did that go?" she asked, sitting on the edge of the lounge chair he was relaxing in.

"Better than I thought." He smiled at her softly. "I was scared of seeing her, but I don't know what I felt."

"Pretty much the same as you felt when you ran into your father, I suspect?"

"She ended our relationship because I was absent. I put my schooling first, and we drifted apart. It destroyed me when she left me, but I deserved it."

"And that's why you don't want a marriage?"

His jaw clenched. "Isn't your career the reason why you don't want a marriage either?"

Adeline's heart skipped a beat. "I suppose. My trust was broken. I almost lost everything."

"You told me you had to switch medical schools because of a bad relationship. Why?"

Adeline sighed and she sat down in the lounge chair next to him.

"I fell in love with one of my professors."

Elias's eyes widened. "Oh."

"Yeah. It was a huge mistake. I fell head over heels for Gregory. Back then I still believed in love and the fairy tale. It was magical, and then I found out he was married."

"And you called it off?" he asked.

"I did. I'm not a home wrecker. I was so brokenhearted and humiliated, but I wasn't going to be the other woman. So I ended it. He was furious, but instead of walking away, he exposed it. He said I seduced him, that I was blackmailing him for high grades. Everyone believed him. I had to leave the school, and I took a year off and reapplied. I learned then to keep myself independent."

"I'm sorry."

"So, yeah. I have something to prove too. At one time I did believe in a happy-ever-after."

"Me too," he said quietly.

Her heart skipped a beat, and she reached out and took his hand. "So you wanted marriage, kids?"

"I thought I did. I convinced myself I didn't, but I do…" He trailed off. His gaze dropped down, and he reached out to touch her belly. That simple, gentle touch caused a warmth that spread through her.

She covered his hand with hers on her belly, and she wasn't that jealous about his ex being so close. He had opened up to her like no one ever had before, and she was opening up to him. Trust was hard-won for her.

This was scaring her.

She got up, putting distance between her and Elias.

Her pulse was racing. This is what she wanted, but she was so afraid if she reached out and took it, it would slip away.

She turned and looked out over the vineyard. The sun was setting over the foothills, giving them a golden glow. She could see the appeal of staying here, but she understood Elias's calling for medicine. She understood it all too well.

It was what drove her too.

"I want to thank you again for coming here and for putting up with this subterfuge," he said.

"It's okay. I wanted to be here for you and your sister." Adeline smiled at him. Her heart was beating just a bit faster. Even though she was fighting her feelings for him, she couldn't help herself. Elias made her body react.

She liked being with him.

"I appreciate that." He got up and stood beside her, gently touching her cheek. Her breathing quickened. She recalled the last time he had touched her so gently. And she wanted to be in his arms.

She wanted to forget all the rules she'd set up to protect her heart from him, and just remember all the ways he had made her feel pleasure. And before she could stop herself, she moved closer to him, his arms were around her and they were kissing again.

That heated kiss that had caused her to give in to him a month ago.

This time it was something more than just lust. More than just that raw need, although that lingered there, but something else was buried deep.

Longing. And she felt it too.

"Uncle Elias?" Manny came across the deck, paused, and looked away, embarrassed. "Sorry, Uncle Elias."

"No need." Elias took a step back and Adeline tried to calm her breathing, regaining her composure from that kiss.

"Dinner is ready. Grandma sent me to find you both."

"We'll be right there."

Manny nodded, still not looking at them as he backed away.

Adeline began to laugh. "Well, I think we've embarrassed your nephew."

"I think so." His eyes were twinkling. "Not that I mind in the least."

His arms went around her again and she pushed him away. "We have to go to dinner."

"Fine," Elias said grudgingly. "I'm not looking

AMY RUTTAN   183

forward to this at all. I haven't seen Aidan yet and I'm not... I don't want to see him."

"You're going to have to eventually see him. I mean...our wedding, for a start," she teased.

Elias shook his head, laughed and took her hand.

She was nervous about the dinner, about their deceit and what was going to happen, but she was willing to try.

All Elias wanted to do was take Adeline back to their room and continue to kiss her. Truth be told, over the last month he had never really stopped thinking about her and their time together. He had tried to keep it to himself because it was better for both of them, professionally.

So he had kept it under wraps as they both dealt with the pregnancy and their work, but being here and seeing her fitting in with his family, it was hard to hold back how he felt about her.

Seeing her care for his sister and his unborn niece made him realize how lucky he was to have met Adeline.

He wanted her, but he was so afraid to hand over his heart to her.

When they got down to the dining room, Rosa and Manny were at the table, as were his parents, and there were two remaining seats for himself and Adeline.

There was no seating for Shea or Aidan.

And seeing that infuriated him.

Aidan was more childish and selfish than he had thought. Too afraid to come and see how much Elias had. A medical career, a fiancée who was a doctor.

She's not your fiancée, though.

And that realization made him sad.

He didn't have Adeline, but he wanted to.

Especially now that he understood her. She'd been through the same as him. She'd fought just as hard and he respected her all the more.

"Sorry we're late," Adeline said.

His father smiled at her. "No matter. We're happy you can be here, Adeline."

Elias pulled out Adeline's chair so she could sit down.

"Well, at least my son still has manners," his father said gruffly.

Elias ignored it. It was his dad's usual comment.

Elias was used to his father criticizing him.

Now, if he started criticizing Adeline, then they would have a problem.

"Are Aidan and Shea not joining us?" Elias asked as he took his seat next to Adeline.

Dad looked up at him. "No. Aidan has work to do."

There was no more that his father was going to say, but Elias knew his brother wasn't hiding away because of work. His brother was hiding away because he was here. Elias hadn't seen him since the day he had caught Shea and Aidan together.

The day that Shea chose Aidan over him.

Elias did not go to the wedding. Not that there was a big wedding.

Shea's marriage into the family had caused a rift, but Elias had always felt that his father blamed him for the rift and not Aidan.

And that was part of the problem. Elias knew that he wasn't the favorite child. He had given up the vineyard. Aidan hadn't. Aidan was the perfect son who upheld all the values his father had.

Only, Elias had the same values.

Hard work. Compassion.

He cared about saving lives.

Yet he was the disappointment.

And there was nothing he could do to change that.

The problem was, he cared too much.

He didn't want to be the disappointing son any longer.

He wanted to make his family proud.

He wanted to make Adeline proud.

He wanted to make his child proud.

Dinner was short and awkward.

Elias's family was nice to her, but she could sense an undercurrent of tension, and it had to do with that rivalry between Elias and his brother, Aidan.

Adeline got the distinct feeling that it wasn't tension about Shea anymore.

It was something deeper.

Elias's father didn't say much, and Rosa seemed uncomfortable. She went to bed early. Adeline tried to help Flora with the dishes, but Flora refused.

So Adeline headed back to the bedroom.

It had been a long day and yesterday had been even longer.

All she wanted to do was go to sleep.

Are you really going to sleep much, lying next to Elias?

Throughout dinner, she kept thinking about that stolen kiss out on the deck. The last time they had kissed like that, it had led to something more.

She had been grateful at the time that Manny had interrupted them, but now everyone was going to bed.

You've got this. Be strong.

Only when it came to Elias, she wasn't strong.

She opened the door to the room and shut it. Elias was half-undressed, wearing his jeans but no shirt. It took her by surprise to see him. She'd forgotten how broad and muscular his chest was, visually, because suddenly she was keenly aware of how his chest felt under her touch.

Her cheeks heated and her body thrummed with need.

Her body was very much aware how it felt to be in his arms.

And she wanted him again.

"I tried to help your mother with the dishes. She refused my help," Adeline said lightly.

Elias smiled slightly. "Yes, she never lets guests do that."

"I'm supposed to be her future daughter-in-law. Wouldn't she want help from me?"

"No. Well, not forever. If we were actually to be married, then she would probably start letting you take over."

Adeline laughed. "That's good to know."

"So your mother makes guests wash dishes, then?"

"No. My mother doesn't either. Of course, my parents have a housekeeper." Adeline sat down on the bed. "You're bothered that your brother didn't come tonight, aren't you?"

Elias frowned. "I don't care. Actually, I'm glad he stayed away."

"Have you always disliked him this much?" she asked.

Elias sighed. "No, but there was always a rivalry. Just competition, but I didn't hate him. He seemed to dislike me, though. Always wanting what I had. Always angry at me. Always trying to gain Dad's affection. Still, I never hated him until…"

"Until he stole Shea."

"Yes, but the thing is, I saw her today and I don't care anymore. It was hard seeing her, I won't lie, but it wasn't as bad as I thought because I realized something in that moment when I saw her."

"What?"

"That I only have eyes for you, Adeline."

Her pulse began to race, and she wasn't sure if she had heard him correctly. "What?"

"I don't care about Shea. We drifted apart a long time ago. You're carrying my baby. That's all that matters."

Her heart began to thump hard, and she stood up. "Elias, I'm not… I…"

"I know. I know. You don't want to get married, we're just going to raise this baby together, but Adeline. I still want you. I still desire you." He closed the distance between them, cupping her face in his hands. His touch lit a fire under her skin. "Once was not enough. I have never stopped thinking about you or that moment in the on-call room. If we can't have it all, why can't we have tonight?"

There was a tiny voice inside her head telling her to run, not to trust him, that he was just using her to let out his frustrated emotions involving his family. But the other part of her, the one she'd been ignoring for the last month, was telling her to take it all.

It reminded her of their time together in the on-call room. When she had just wanted him out of her system and had thought once would be enough. She had been wrong, because she'd thought about it too. So many times.

She remembered how good it felt to have him inside her.

To be one with him. She felt needy thinking of him, thinking of his kisses.

And it wouldn't hurt to taste that temptation again. Kissing him out on the deck had already whetted her appetite, and she wanted more.

"Elias," she whispered. "We can't."

"We can't, or we shouldn't?" he asked huskily, and before she could let the rational side of her brain take over, she kissed him, lighting the same fire that she felt every time he was around.

The same fire of desire that hadn't burned out, no matter how many times she tried to put it out.

She wanted Elias.

She wanted to feel him again and have nothing between them.

Just the two of them. Together.

Here.

Now.

This was what she needed more than anything. The more she denied it, the more real it became. She was in love with Elias Garcia. She was in love with a man who didn't want a happy-ever-after either. Just like she didn't.

You're a liar. You want a happy-ever-after. Don't deny it.

Which was true. She wanted it all. Her dream job, her baby, a family and Elias.

"I've missed you, Adeline," he murmured as he kissed her neck.

"I've been here all along."

He smiled at her and touched her face. "I've missed your kisses."

Elias's hands were hot on her skin. There was no more need for words. They both wanted the same thing.

They sank onto the bed, her body humming with excitement as they made fast work of their clothes. Soon there was nothing between them. His hands branded her flesh with his touch. His kisses were deep, possessive.

Adeline wanted to touch him everywhere. She wanted him to feel as much pleasure as he was giving her.

"Adeline," he moaned against her neck. "You're the only one I want."

Same.

Only she didn't say that thought out loud.

She couldn't. She was afraid.

Elias's hot kisses trailed over her body. Down her neck, over her breasts, making her body arch, wanting more and more. No longer wanting to wait. She needed him inside her, possessing her.

He entered her and she cried out as he filled her. No one else had ever made her feel this way.

Adeline was lost to him.

She only wanted him.

He'd broken down all her walls and it terrified her.

She never wanted this night to end. She wanted this moment to last forever. Only, forever scared her.

It wasn't long before both of them came together, and as he held her close, tears stung her eyes. She clung to him, not wanting him to see her cry, but unable to stop all the conflicting emotions coursing through her.

The emotions that were telling her she could have forever. If she wanted it.

CHAPTER ELEVEN

AN URGENT KNOCKING roused Adeline out of her sleep. The sun was streaming in the window and she was curled up against Elias, who was sleeping still.

"Uncle Elias, Dr. Turner!" Manny's voice was panicked on the other side of the door.

"Elias." Adeline shook him awake. "It's Manny!"

Elias startled awake and jumped out of bed, pulling on his clothes, as Adeline did the same.

Elias dashed across the room and opened the door. "Manny, what's the matter?"

"Mom went into labor, but it rained last night, and a road is washed out. The ambulance can't get here and something's wrong."

"I'm on my way, Manny." Adeline grabbed her medical kit and dashed out the door to Rosa's room.

A terrified Flora was with Rosa, who was in agony and incoherent.

"Rosa, it's Adeline. When did your contractions start?" Adeline was washing her hands in the en suite bathroom.

"I don't know… I woke up in pain," Rosa cried out.

"Manny came to get me," Flora said.

Elias entered the room, and Adeline could feel his worry. "What can I do?"

"Support her, Elias," Adeline whispered. "I don't know what's going on, but we need to get an ambulance here. I have nothing to monitor the baby… I don't know what's going to happen."

Elias took Rosa's hands as Rosa cried.

"Manny, maybe you should wait outside?" Adeline suggested.

Manny nodded. "I'll keep calling for help."

Adeline smiled encouragingly. "Yes. Do that."

She grabbed an ottoman and sat at the foot of the bed to check, and she could see the baby crowning. This baby was coming, fast and furious.

"Rosa, do you feel any contractions?" Adeline asked.

"A bit…" She moaned.

"On the next one I need you to push for me." Adeline got up and placed her hand on Rosa's belly, feeling for it herself. "Okay. Push. Get angry, do it, and push for me."

Elias climbed behind Rosa to hold her shoulders as Flora helped support her daughter's legs. Adeline watched the baby.

There was more blood than she would have liked, but there was no stopping this baby. She was on her way.

"Okay, push again!" Adeline shouted.

The baby's shoulders were delivered first, and then it only took one half push and the little baby girl was born. Silent.

"Why isn't my baby crying?" Rosa called weakly.

Elias leaped up and helped Adeline rub the baby with a towel, trying to stimulate the little girl. There was a small cry and Rosa smiled, but the baby wasn't breathing well, and there was a bluish tinge to her little lips.

Adeline glanced up at Elias, and he knew that this baby would need extra oxygen.

"Uncle Aidan got hold of Air Ambulance," Manny said, rushing back into the room. His eyes widened on his little sister, barely crying and being held by Elias. Then Aidan entered the room. Elias stiffened at the sight of his brother.

Aidan's gaze locked on Elias holding the little girl. There was a palpable tension, but they didn't say anything to each other.

Elias handed his niece to Rosa.

"She's beautiful," Flora cried.

Adeline's heart sank, because the baby needed urgent help. She was glad Air Ambulance was on its way.

"Rosa, we have to get the baby to the hospital," Elias said gently.

Rosa's eyes filled with tears as she glanced down at her daughter. "I know. I want you to go with Gabrielle, Elias. Please."

Aidan stated, "Rosa, I promised Jeffery that I would accompany you to the hospital."

"I should go. I'm the neonatologist," Elias snapped. "I'm the one with pediatric resuscitation training."

Aidan's eyes narrowed. "I haven't forgotten."

"Enough!" Flora snapped. "Elias will go with Gabriella! Aidan, you can stay with Rosa while Adeline takes care of her and we wait for the air ambulance."

Aidan looked at her, but barely. His cheeks were flushed because he'd been chastised by his mother. Adeline could hear the helicopter outside.

"I'll go let them in," Aidan stated. "Come on, Manny."

Manny followed.

"Elias?" Adeline motioned for Elias to come closer while Rosa and Flora doted over Gabrielle. "Do you think there's room on that helicopter for Rosa?"

"I don't know. Why?"

Adeline showed him. "She's hemorrhaging. I can't get it to stop. I suspect a rupture. She's vulnerable after her C-section."

Elias went pale. "I'll go speak to the paramedics. Do what you can."

Adeline nodded. She was remaining calm, because she didn't want to alarm Rosa or Flora, but Adeline knew. Rosa had had a large baby and a previous C-section. The placenta wasn't releasing, and Adeline suspected a tear.

The paramedics came in the room with an incubator. And thankfully they also had a stretcher.

"We have room to take them both, but only room for one other person to accompany them to the hospital."

Elias glanced at Adeline. "You need to go."

"You're the pediatrician," Adeline said.

"There are NICU doctors there at the Napa hospital. You need to go and take care of Rosa." Elias was right. She could do the surgery to fix the repair.

Elias helped the paramedics get the baby in the incubator and on oxygen, while Adeline kept an eye on Rosa, who was becoming weaker.

Adeline stood up. "Uncontrolled bleeding. We need to start fluids and oxygen."

The paramedics nodded, and Adeline stood back as they lifted Rosa onto the stretcher. Adeline helped as they stabilized her, and she followed the stretcher out to the helicopter. Elias was waiting, the baby's incubator already loaded.

His father and Aidan stood close by with Manny.

Rosa was in distress.

"I'll follow in the car," Elias said to Adeline. He looked broken. "Just save my sister."

Adeline nodded. "I will."

They loaded Rosa into the helicopter and Adeline followed. The doors were shut, and she slipped on the headphones.

The helicopter whirred to life and began to lift off.

"Adeline," Rosa murmured. Adeline took her hand and held it.

"I'm here," she reassured Rosa.

"Don't let me die."

Adeline's throat clenched and tears stung her eyes. "I won't."

She would make sure of it.

Elias felt like his heart was breaking as he watched that helicopter take off. His mother had buried her head in his father's shoulder, and his father's arm was around Manny. Aidan stood there scowling, and Elias didn't have the patience to deal with him.

He had to get to the hospital.

As soon as the helicopter was away, he turned and marched back into the house. He had to put his shoes on, grab his keys and get himself to the hospital. He had to be there for Rosa and Adeline.

Although he wouldn't be able to assist in the surgery.

"Where are you going?" Aidan demanded, following him in.

"Where do you think I'm going?" Elias asked. "I'm going to the hospital."

"What? As support for Rosa? You haven't been home in two years! I've been looking after Rosa and Manny since you stopped coming around. When Jeffery was away on business, I'm the one that stepped in while you flounced off to medical school. I was always here."

Elias glared at his brother. "Flounced off to medical school? Hardly. I followed my dream. You always wanted to run this vineyard, so I let you have it!"

Aidan smirked. "Oh, you graciously let me have it."

"Yes. And how did you repay me, brother? You married the woman I loved."

"I didn't steal her," Aidan spat out viciously. "You abandoned her like you did the rest of us. I was there when you weren't."

"We grew apart. I didn't abandon her!"

"Yes, you did. You can't accept when you're wrong." Aidan got right up in his face, infuriating him.

Elias pushed Aidan away and Aidan shoved him into the wall. Elias had been waiting so long to do this, but the thing was, the fight wasn't about Shea anymore.

He didn't care that Aidan had married Shea. He hadn't for some time. It was an excuse.

He was angry about losing his brother.

He was angry that he had lost his family all this time, and that wasn't Aidan's fault. It was his own. He was mad at himself.

Elias didn't want to fight, but it was apparent that Aidan did.

"Stop it!" his father shouted, coming into the room, breaking them apart. "Stop it! The pair of you, behaving like animals when your sister's life is in danger."

Aidan let Elias go and walked away from him, leaving Elias leaning against the wall.

"What is the matter with you?" Jimeno demanded.

"Nothing is the matter with me," Elias snapped. "He's the one who said I was abandoning the family."

"You did," Jimeno said, but then he turned on Aidan. "You don't think that Elias has a right to be mad at you? You stole the woman he was supposed to marry. I know they had drifted apart and were no longer in love and that it all worked out, but you always had to have what Elias had. Thankfully, Elias has found a new fiancée, but you broke his trust."

Elias was shocked by his father's words. Then the guilt overtook him.

He was done trying to prove himself to them.

"Adeline is not my fiancée. She is my work partner and is carrying my child, but she's not my fiancée," Elias said.

Aidan smirked. "Always trying to be better than me and you're still the same, Elias."

"You're right, but I'm not the same, Aidan. Not anymore."

"Quiet. The pair of you. You're brothers but you act like enemies. You're both a disappointment to me right now." Jimeno glared at Aidan before turning to Elias.

"Elias, I may not have agreed with all your choices in life, but you clearly care for Adeline. If she is pregnant with your child, you need to make this right."

Elias didn't say anything else. He didn't know what to think. All he knew was he had to get to the hospital. He would have NICU privileges and he wanted to make sure that Adeline was supported.

"I'm going to the hospital," Elias grumbled. He headed down the hall, then quickly cleaned up, changed and got his wallet and keys.

Aidan followed him. "You can't drive to Napa."

"I may have been away for two years, but I know how to drive," Elias grunted.

"No, your rental won't get through the road closure, but I know the new backroads and my truck can handle it. I'll drive you." It was a peace offering in Aidan's own stubborn way, and as much as Elias didn't want to accept it, Aidan was right.

It would be better if Aidan drove.

He nodded. "Thank you."

Aidan's eyes widened as if he was surprised by the thank-you. "I'll bring the truck around."

Elias finished gathering what he needed and then headed outside. Jimeno, Flora, Manny and Shea were already there. Shea was holding on to Aidan and he was whispering something to her.

The way she looked at Aidan was a way she had never looked at him, and Elias couldn't recall if he had ever looked at Shea like that either.

"Call me as soon as you have news," Flora said, her voice shaking as she hugged him.

"I will, Mom. I promise," Elias said.

Elias gave Manny a hug and then got into Aidan's truck. Aidan climbed in and drove away from the family estate.

Elias could barely look at his brother, but felt he had to break the ice somehow.

"So, why didn't you come to dinner last night?"

Aidan shrugged. "I thought I would give you time with the family. I see them all the time and I didn't think you wanted to see me."

"No. You're right. I didn't." Which was true, but deep down, he'd missed his brother. He regretted the way that they had been so competitive in their late teens. The way they had grown apart and hated each other for all this time.

It seemed like such a waste.

"See, then why ask why I wasn't there?" Aidan shook his head. "You're so stubborn!"

"You're just like Dad!" Elias snapped back.

Aidan glared and then laughed. "Yeah, I suppose I am."

Elias found himself laughing too.

"Except I could never measure up to you, and Mom and Dad have never let Shea or me forget what we did to you." Aidan sighed. "It's just you…"

"I was never around."

Aidan nodded. "You left us both. You went off to higher learning and you looked down your nose at the rest of us who worked the land. You made Dad and me feel less than you. No one could hold a candle to you and your great surgical career."

Elias felt guilty, because his brother wasn't wrong. When he was younger, he had looked down his nose at the work his father and brother did and the generations that had come before him. All the blood, sweat and tears that went into the land. He had thought he was above all that.

Above getting his hands dirty.

He'd been an idiot. He could see that now.

He'd hurt his father and his brother.

He'd been wrong.

"I was wrong back then." Elias looked at him quickly. "I'm sorry."

Aidan's eyes widened. "I think that Dad was hard on you because he wanted you to push yourself in your medical career. There were no shortcuts to success. You worked hard or you didn't eat."

Elias nodded. "And he was hard on you because you were taking over the land. You have to be tough to work it and make it successful."

"So we've spent all these years thinking each other had it easier, when he was really riding us both." Aidan smiled at him and Elias nodded, grinning back.

"Yeah, only we were both too stubborn to see that."

"As stubborn as he is," Aidan said.

They rode the rest of the way in silence. Things still weren't resolved between them, but they were better.

They were on the right road.

Elias could adapt.

He was a surgeon. And being a surgeon meant a lot of adaptability. If he could only convince Adeline how important it was to do the same.

"You trained with Dr. Wilder in San Diego?" the head of obstetrics, Dr. Lyttle, asked as they scrubbed in while Rosa was being prepped in the operating room.

"I still am," Adeline stated.

"I'm glad you're here," Dr. Lyttle admitted as

she continued to scrub. "And here I thought it was going to be a quiet Sunday."

Adeline smiled. "Thank you for allowing me surgical privileges."

"Of course. It's not every day we see a uterine rupture, and I'm glad to have the extra hand. Your sister-in-law has lost a lot of blood."

"She's not my sister-in-law."

Not yet.

"Oh, the patient said you were."

Adeline shook her head. "She's a bit of a matchmaker. Her brother is my colleague in San Diego. It's a long story, but there's no family relation. I can operate."

And Adeline wanted to be there for Rosa, just as she had promised when Rosa was crashing before the ambulance came.

Don't let me die.

That voice so small, so haunting, had lodged in her brain, and she wanted to be with Rosa every step of the way. She didn't want to let the Garcia family down.

She didn't want to let Elias down.

Adeline finished scrubbing in and headed into the operating room, following Dr. Lyttle. A scrub nurse helped her get on a gown and gloves.

"This patient is thirty-five-year-old Rosa Adler. Spontaneously delivered a ten-pound infant today during a VBAC. Her last child was born fifteen years ago in a crash C-section. There was a lot of bleeding after birth and the placenta did not detach. Suspected uterine tear, possible rupture," Dr. Lyttle said, informing the residents, nurses and other staff in the operating room. "Dr. Turner will be leading this surgery, as per the patient's wishes."

"Thank you." Adeline took a deep breath. The energy in the room was off and for the first time, she needed a moment. "Could we all just take a minute and meditate? This is a life in our hands."

She closed her eyes and dropped her head. She just needed a moment and Rosa was stable, for now.

This was something Dr. Wilder never did, but right now Adeline needed to ground herself. She needed to connect and change the flow of energy to calm her nerves as she operated on the sister of the man she loved.

And she did love Elias.

"Thanks, everyone. Let's save a life." Adeline stepped up to the operating table, and the scrub nurse handed her the scalpel.

Adeline knew what to do. She'd been so focused on Dr. Wilder teaching her for years, but really, she'd assimilated all she needed to know.

There was still more she could learn, but for the first time, she was confident here.

Here, at this table, she was an attending surgeon. She drained everything else from her mind. Her pregnancy, Elias, the spot with Dr. Wilder, TTP.

She focused on Rosa. She focused on the patient she was going to save. She had never been so sure about anything in her life.

There weren't many things she was sure about, but she was sure of this.

And she could do it.

Elias was pacing in the hall. He wasn't allowed into the operating room, so to kill time during the surgery, he went to the NICU to check on his niece, Gabrielle, where he was given access. He put on a gown, mask and gloves.

It reminded him of when Manny had been born.

Only then, he'd been a fifteen-year-old boy, and that had been the moment when he decided that he was going to be a neonatologist and a pediatrician.

It was the need to prove himself to his father, to his brother, to show them he was worth more than what they thought of him, that had made him push himself so hard to get a place in Dr. Wilder's program, but this was where his true passion lay. The NICU, working with these ill babies. This is where he belonged. He could see that now.

He didn't need to keep chasing the biggest and the best things.

He'd had it all along.

He didn't need that spot.

And as soon as he got to San Diego he was going to give it up. He was going to step back. Adeline should be the one who had the fellowship with Dr. Wilder.

She had a passion for birth.

For saving both mother and child, connected, when they were most vulnerable, and he was so thankful that he had listened to Adeline.

That he had listened to her instincts.

He didn't even want to think what about would have happened if they hadn't been there for Rosa and sweet little Gabrielle.

It was too terrifying to dwell on and it made him feel so guilty that he hadn't been home in so long. That he had walked away from his family because his pride had been hurt.

What an idiot he had been.

He made his way to the incubator and smiled down at his niece all hooked up. She had dark hair like her mother.

"Gabrielle," Elias whispered. And he reached into the incubator to take her tiny fist, balled around a sensor.

"You're Dr. Garcia?"

Elias spun around to see a gowned doctor standing behind him. "Yes."

"I'm Dr. Richardson. Head of neonatology. I've been informed your sister is still in surgery, so I'm hoping I can talk to you about your niece?"

"Of course, Dr. Richardson." Elias's heart sank.

"We want to airlift the baby to San Francisco. As you are aware, the baby had a PDA, but it's quite large. We're frankly amazed she survived birth."

Elias swallowed the lump in his throat. "You want to do heart surgery on her?"

Dr. Richardson nodded. "The children's hospital in San Francisco is better equipped to do that procedure, and the pediatric cardiologist is one of the best in California. We need to send the baby right away. We can't wait for the mother to give us permission, but we did get hold of the baby's father and he told us to do whatever it took."

"My brother-in-law is correct, and I'll make sure that Rosa knows what's going on with the baby when she gets out of surgery."

"Thank you, Dr. Garcia. We do need someone to accompany the baby to San Francisco."

"My brother, Aidan Garcia, can," Elias offered.

"That's great."

Elias stood back to watch as Dr. Richardson and his team prepared everything they needed to get Gabrielle back into a medical helicopter. Elias left the NICU and made his way down to the waiting room, where Aidan was pacing up and down.

Aidan glanced up. "What?"

"The baby needs to be transferred to San Francisco. Now."

"Why? What's wrong?" Aidan asked, panicked.

"Gabrielle's heart. She needs surgery and they
aren't able to do that here. Not as well as it can
be done in San Francisco."

Aidan scrubbed a hand over his face.

"You need to go with the baby to San Francisco. I'll stay here and let Rosa know what's
going on, but someone needs to go with Gabrielle
until Jeffery gets back to California."

"You're the doctor. Shouldn't you go?" Aidan
asked.

Elias swallowed his pride. "I may be a doctor,
but I am her uncle. There is nothing I could do
there. They wouldn't let me. Go, keep Gabrielle
safe. Rosa trusts you. Jeffery trusts you and it
should be you. I'll take care of Rosa."

Aidan's hard expression softened. "Thank
you."

Elias clapped him on the shoulder. "They're
waiting for you."

Aidan nodded and made his way to the NICU
to travel with Gabrielle.

Elias's heart was breaking as he worried about
what was going to happen next and how he would
break it to Rosa. And he couldn't stop thinking
about how it would feel if Adeline was on the
table with the dreaded TTP. What if it was his
child who was dying? What if it was his child
who needed surgery?

Could he handle it?

He could handle things like this as a surgeon when his family wasn't involved, but this, this was torture.

His heart was breaking.

And he was scared. He sat down in a chair, his head in his hands, and he felt like he was on the verge of breaking.

So many wasted years.

Not wasted. And you did the right thing.

Although he felt like a fool for having been away so long, and now he wasn't sure his sister or his niece were going to survive this ordeal.

Adeline is with Rosa. Everything will be okay.

"Elias?" Adeline's voice came from the doorway.

He looked up and she was in her scrubs.

"Tell me," he said, his voice shaking.

Adeline smiled. "She'll be fine."

Elias smiled, too, and leaped up to kiss Adeline.

Adeline laughed. "That's not usually how patients' families greet their surgeons."

"Maybe it should be," he teased and kissed her again.

Adeline looked at him gently. "She had a uterine rupture. The scar from Manny's birth didn't hold during Gabrielle's fast, forceful birth. I had no choice but to do a hysterectomy. There was too much damage, but she'll survive. How is the baby?"

"They're airlifting her to San Francisco. Her heart...they need to send her to the children's hospital in San Francisco where pediatric surgeons can operate on her to save her."

Adeline frowned. "I'm so sorry."

"I have to tell Rosa."

"Who went with the baby?" Adeline asked.

"Aidan."

"Aidan?" she asked, confused.

"Aidan drove me up here. We...talked. I don't think things are perfect, but they're better."

Adeline reached down and took his hand. It felt so good having her hand on his. "I see. I'm glad."

"I'm going to call the family."

Adeline nodded. "Call them and then I'll take you up to see Rosa. We're going to have to head back to San Francisco sooner rather than later. We have one more case left there. Dr. Wilder is counting on us."

"Yes." Although Elias didn't really care about what Dr. Wilder thought of him, but he knew it was important to Adeline, and he wanted to be close to his niece. He had privileges at the children's hospital in San Francisco. He might not be able to do anything to help his niece, but he could be there, in the NICU.

Adeline left to change out of her borrowed scrubs and Elias pulled out his cell phone. Once the family was here for Rosa, he and Adeline could take Aidan's truck back to the vineyard, grab their rental and head to San Francisco, where he was going to tell Dr. Wilder that he was out.

He didn't want the fellowship.

He knew where he belonged.

CHAPTER TWELVE

ADELINE WAS EXHAUSTED from the long surgery, and they had to wait until Rosa was out of the post anesthesia care unit so Elias could tell her what was going on with Gabrielle.

Aidan had updated the family that Gabrielle was going into surgery in the morning but was stable and that he was staying at the hospital until Jeffery got there.

Jeffery was on a plane and would be landing in San Francisco early tomorrow morning. Rosa was devastated, but Manny and her parents were there to comfort her.

Elias had promised Rosa that he would return to San Francisco and take care of Jeffery and Gabrielle until she was released.

So by the time they returned to the vineyard, packed up their stuff and headed back out on the road, it was midnight.

It had been a long, grueling day, but Adeline was eager to get back to San Francisco. She knew that Elias needed to be with his niece, and Adeline wanted to get back to work. Being around Elias's family made her homesick. She still hadn't been to see her mother.

Nor had she heard about the genetic testing, but that could wait until they got back to San Diego.

"I want to thank you again," Elias said after a while.

"For what?"

"For saving my sister's life. If you hadn't been there… I don't even want to think about it. You're a talented surgeon and you saved her."

A blush tinged her cheeks. "Thank you."

"You're welcome." He glanced at her, smiling. "You know, I don't think there's anything left that you need to learn from Dr. Wilder. You're fully capable of being an attending anywhere. You were an attending."

That comment caught her off guard.

Was he trying to trick her?

He's not trying to trick you. It's been a long day.

"Thanks," she said, and she smiled, but this time it was forced. It was fake, because she couldn't get that niggling thought out of her head that he was saying this to confuse her. When they had met, she and Elias had been in competition, and the part of her that warned and protected her from getting hurt was telling her that Elias was *still* her competition.

That he wanted that position for himself.

Yet the other part of her, the part that had let him in, was telling her she was being foolish. Elias wasn't like that.

She pulled out her phone and saw a text.

"It's Dr. Wilder," she said.

"Oh?" he asked.

"She flew into San Francisco. My twin-to-twin transfusion patient needs to be delivered tomorrow morning. Early." Adeline groaned.

"You need to take care of yourself."

"I know that," she snapped.

"You have more than just yourself to take care of. You're pregnant."

"I know." She was annoyed that he was reminding her of the obvious. He was right, but she knew this surgery would be the surgery that would prove herself to Dr. Wilder.

Haven't you proved yourself enough?

And that was something she had never thought about before. She had been working with Dr. Wilder for a year. She had given up an attending spot to work with Dr. Wilder. Essentially becoming a student again. Doing everything, learning all she could. She had turned down many positions during this year.

She could become an attending anywhere.

She could have her own practice.

Dr. Wilder didn't have the cure for TTP. No one did, but Dr. Wilder had so many clinical trials on the go. If anyone was going to cure that awful genetic disease, it was going to be Dr. Wilder, and Adeline wanted to be a part of that.

Who says you won't be the one to do it?

She shook that thought away and tried to make herself comfortable, listening to the sound of the car rolling down the highway. Adeline leaned her head against the car door and watched as San Francisco's city lights came into view. She closed her eyes to quiet her mind, which was racing.

Only the best ever got in with Dr. Wilder. And she wanted to be the best.

Do you?

It made her stomach knot. She didn't know anymore.

Maybe you're scared?

And she was. She was scared.

Elias parked the SUV in front of their rental apartment and then picked up Adeline out of the passenger seat with ease. She was fast asleep, and she only stirred slightly as he picked her up. He carried her inside, took her straight to her bed and laid her down gently, covering her.

She looked so peaceful.

He hated to disturb her. She had saved his sister's life and he would be eternally grateful, but he wished that she wasn't so hell-bent on being Dr. Wilder's lackey for the rest of her career. Adeline was so talented.

She could easily take a head of obstetrics job at any hospital she wanted.

People liked her. Patients liked her. She deserved so much more.

She was brilliant.

She didn't need Dr. Wilder and he wished she could see that.

She had exactly what she needed, but she was too scared to try.

Aren't you scared to try?

Elias sighed and shut the door to her bedroom. His phone buzzed and he answered the call.

"Dr. Garcia speaking."

"Garcia, it's Wilder. I've been trying to get hold of Dr. Turner. She hasn't responded."

"She delivered a baby this morning and did a grueling uterine rupture repair in Napa today. We just got back to San Francisco. Adeline is sleeping, but I can wake her…"

"No. Don't bother waking her. These twins need to be delivered in the next hour. The mother has preeclampsia. Can you come and assist me? You can fill me in on the details of this surgery Dr. Turner performed."

"Sure thing, Dr. Wilder." Elias ended the call.

He was tired too, but he wasn't as tired as Adeline and he wasn't pregnant. He could down some coffee and be ready to go. Dr. Wilder just needed an assist and he wanted to be there for the twins. They would need extra support as well.

It was apparent to him that Dr. Wilder didn't care who was there. Even though Adeline was far more qualified.

And Adeline needed her sleep.

Elias quickly changed, left a note and locked up. He walked to the hospital and met up with Dr. Wilder at the operating room, where she was scrubbing in next to Dr. Spiner.

"So, Garcia, tell me about this delivery and surgery that Dr. Turner attended to," Dr. Wilder said.

"It was my sister. It was a VBAC, but the baby was large and was delivered quickly, in barely an hour. My niece had a PDA and was airlifted to the Napa hospital before her transfer to the children's hospital here in San Francisco."

"Tell me about the rupture," Dr. Wilder said. "Once the baby is born, it's not my concern."

That struck Elias the wrong way. It was clinical and coldhearted.

Arrogant.

"Dr. Turner suspected a rupture and we airlifted the patient to the hospital, where Dr. Turner led the surgery to repair the damage by doing a hysterectomy."

"She's fantastic!" Dr. Spiner announced out loud. "If you're not careful, Dr. Wilder, I'll steal her and Dr. Garcia away."

Dr. Wilder looked at Dr. Spiner with curiosity. "Is that a fact?"

"They're both talented surgeons and make a

wonderful team, and San Francisco is a great place to raise a baby," Dr. Spiner announced cheerily.

Elias stomach dropped to the soles of his shoes and Dr. Wilder looked at him, her eyebrow cocked.

"A baby?" she asked Elias.

"Rats. Sorry, Dr. Garcia, I wasn't supposed to spill the beans. I thought Dr. Wilder knew." Dr. Spiner finished and headed into the operating room.

Elias felt like he couldn't swallow as he continued to scrub in.

"That certainly explains her exhaustion," Dr. Wilder said quietly. "She has to take care of herself. She wouldn't want to put any extra stress on herself or the baby."

"She is taking care of herself," Elias defended her. "And she is getting rest."

"Is that why I was given genetic test results for her?"

"You were given the results?" Elias asked, confused.

Dr. Wilder nodded. "It was ordered on one of my lab request forms, so the lab sent it to me via email. I was hoping to see Dr. Turner tonight to give her the results."

Elias wanted to know what the results were, but he had no right. He wasn't her fiancé. He wasn't her significant other. He was just the father of the baby, and the genetic tests, although they might affect the pregnancy, had nothing to do with him. He had no legal rights to her information.

"Well, I hope after your harrowing day with your sister that you'll be able to work tonight, Dr. Garcia. I need assistance to deliver these babies, and I'm sure you will find it particularly fascinating how twin-to-twin transfusion syndrome affects the different twins."

"Yes, Dr. Wilder."

Dr. Wilder headed into the operating room and Elias finished scrubbing up. He was angry with himself for letting news of the pregnancy slip to Dr. Spiner, and he had meant to tell Adeline that he had accidentally told Dr. Spiner about it. Yet never in a million years had he thought that Dr. Spiner would spill the beans to Dr. Wilder.

But Dr. Spiner seemed to be a chatty, bubbly type of surgeon.

And he hoped that Dr. Wilder wouldn't use the pregnancy against Adeline. Dr. Wilder had made it clear to all those who were vying for a position in her program that studying maternal-fetal medicine was not for the faint of heart. It took up a lot of time.

There was no time for a personal life. No time for family.

And that was one of the reasons that had drawn him to vie for the spot. He hadn't wanted all of that. He hadn't wanted a personal life. His life had been his work. That's what he'd done since medical school. He'd been running from his pain.

And then he had met Adeline, and everything had changed. Now he wanted it all. He wanted Adeline and the baby, and he wanted to work here in San Francisco so that he could be close to his family.

The thing was, he wasn't sure that it had changed for Adeline. She was so single-minded about winning this fellowship. It was what she wanted.

It's what she had always wanted, and he wasn't sure that *he* was enough for her.

Adeline woke up early the next morning, because she had set her alarm after Dr. Wilder had texted her. She showered quickly and went to check on Elias, but Elias wasn't there, and it looked as though his bed hadn't even been slept in.

Which was strange, but then she thought that he was probably at the children's hospital with Gabrielle. Which made sense, and if Dr. Wilder asked about him, Adeline would tell her that Elias needed to be with his family.

Adeline gathered everything she needed for her day at the hospital, although her body was protesting. She was still exhausted from yesterday.

She hadn't told Elias that after the successful surgery on Rosa, she had been offered a position to be an attending in obstetrics in Napa. It was tempting—they had offered her a lot—but she was so close to getting everything she wanted.

Is this everything you want, though?

And that thought surprised her, because there had never been a moment in her entire career when she had second-guessed this fellowship. Except recently, when she had met Elias and fallen pregnant and everything had changed in her life.

She shook her head as she continued her walk to the hospital from the apartment. She couldn't let herself think this way.

Elias didn't want a family.

He barely wanted to be around the family he had, and she hadn't been home in a few months. She hadn't even told her mother she was pregnant.

Adeline paused at the top of the street, looking back down at the park. The sun was rising, and San Francisco was waking up. It was a clear day and from where she was standing at the top of this street, she could see the peaks of the Golden Gate Bridge rising over the city.

Even though she visited home, she hadn't ever really been home.

She'd forgotten how much she loved it here.

How peaceful it made her feel.

Ever since she went away to school, when she had decided to devote her life to medicine and helping women, Adeline hadn't really taken a moment to live, to breathe.

It was like that day in the operating room.

Right before she operated on Rosa. She took that moment to breathe and it was calming.

She'd been going for so long. Running herself ragged.

This is what you want, though.

Dr. Wilder would teach her everything. Elias might think that Adeline was capable enough, but she wasn't. She wasn't ready to take the leap yet. She needed to learn more. She needed to save more lives.

She wasn't ready.

Yes, you are.

Adeline sighed and continued on her way to the hospital. She didn't want to be late for Dr. Wilder, who didn't like it when her staff were tardy. She entered the hospital and made her way up to the obstetrics floor.

She wanted to check on her patient before they prepped her for surgery.

After she put her stuff in a locker and got into her scrubs, she headed for the nurses' station and looked through the clipboards for her patient's file.

"Um, do you know where room nine's file is?"

"Room nine?" the nurse asked, confused.

"Yeah, the twin-to-twin transfusion patient. I did that surgery a couple of days ago, but Dr. Wilder texted that we were going to operate this morning and deliver the babies."

"Oh, Dr. Wilder and Dr. Garcia delivered those

babies early this morning," the nurse said. "The mother is currently upstairs in the NICU with the twins."

Adeline shook her head, not quite hearing what the nurse was saying. "Sorry, what?"

"The babies were delivered about two a.m." The nurse picked up another file and headed off.

Adeline just stood there, stunned. Not sure what to think.

Elias had delivered her patient's babies with Dr. Wilder.

See? What did I tell you?

Adeline swallowed the hard lump that had formed in her throat and she made her way up to the NICU, because she had to see this for herself.

When she got there, she saw her patient in a wheelchair with her husband. Elias was standing next to the incubators and was speaking with the parents.

Adeline felt nauseous. She felt like the rug had been pulled out from under her.

Why hadn't she been contacted?

Why had Dr. Wilder chosen Elias instead of her? Adeline was the one who had assisted with that twin-to-twin surgery. She was the one with more experience. She was the OB-GYN.

She was the one who had been the primary surgeon here in San Francisco. None of it made any sense and she felt betrayed by Elias.

He had stolen her patient. He had just let her

sleep and taken her surgery. She had thought they were becoming friends. She had thought they were falling for each other.

She had thought she could have more with him.

She had thought she could give him her heart.

She had thought the crazy competitive drive was over. How wrong she'd been.

It was like a gut punch.

A punch in the heart.

Adeline headed down to the obstetrics floor. And as she made her way back to the nurses' station to see what she could find out, still stunned and feeling hurt and worried, she saw Dr. Wilder was there.

"Good morning, Dr. Turner," Dr. Wilder said, barely looking up at her.

"Good morning, Dr. Wilder. I see the twin-to-twin patient came through her surgery well." She could barely swallow.

"She did. We had to deliver early this morning. I tried to call you, but there was no answer. However, Dr. Garcia answered his phone and was a great help."

"That's wonderful," Adeline said, but she could barely get the words out of her mouth.

"Can I speak with you a moment, Dr. Turner?" Dr. Wilder said, which sent a shiver of dread down Adeline's spine.

"Of course." It was not like she was going to say no.

Dr. Wilder walked to a private room and opened the door.

Adeline headed inside, shutting the door behind her. She was worried she was going to get chastised for not being there early this morning, for missing that call. She felt awful about it, because this was her career. This was what she was working towards, and she had never missed a day yet.

Dr. Wilder took a seat and Adeline sat down as well.

"So, first things first. I have your genetic test results." Dr. Wilder reached into her pocket and held out a slip of paper.

"You have my test results?" Adeline asked, confused. "Why?"

"The lab request paperwork had my practice address and name, so the lab sent me the results, thinking that you were my patient."

Adeline's cheeks heated with embarrassment. "My apologies, Dr. Wilder."

"Don't apologize. That is an important disease to be aware of. Who in your family was afflicted with it?"

"My mother. She's had multiple flare-ups of TTP since my birth, but it was only recently that they found the gene and deemed it genetic. I thought it was time that I got tested."

Dr. Wilder. "A smart thing, too. Well, I'm pleased to report that you do not have a genetic predisposition for it, which is good for you, given that you're what…five weeks pregnant?"

Adeline's heart stopped.

And she could feel the blood drain away from her face. "Pardon?"

"Dr. Spiner informed me that you are pregnant. He was trying to convince me that he could steal you away and that San Francisco is a good place to raise a family."

The lump in her throat got larger and her pulse was racing. "And how did…how did Dr. Spiner know? I didn't tell anyone."

"Dr. Garcia I believe told him," Dr. Wilder said offhandedly.

Her heart was crushed then. It shattered into a million pieces.

She shouldn't have put her trust in Elias. She shouldn't have let him into her life, let him into her heart. She tried her best to control the tears that were stinging her eyes. This was what Gregory had done—thrown her under the bus to protect himself.

She'd been a fool listening to her heart.

"As you know, my fellowship is a grueling four years. Successful candidates for maternal-fetal medicine need to be available twenty-four hours a day, seven days a week. They have to master many procedures, take part in my clinical research and travel where I can't. You're going to have a baby, Dr. Turner. You won't be available to work the hours that I would require. That's why I offered the position to Dr. Garcia."

"You offered it to Dr. Garcia?" Adeline asked, clearing her throat and feeling defeated. All the years she had spent, all the offers she had turned down, it had been for nothing.

Nothing.

And here she was, with a broken heart again.

"I did offer it to him, but he turned me down. So I called Dr. Simpson and offered the position to her. She's not my first choice, obviously, but she's not pregnant and she is available to do the work. Maybe in a few years when your child is older and you have a few more years under your belt, you can apply again."

Adeline nodded. "Thank you, Dr. Wilder."

Dr. Wilder got up and left. Adeline sat there in shock. She was shocked that Dr. Simpson had gotten the position and enraged that after all of this, Elias had turned down Dr. Wilder.

He had sabotaged her career, her dreams, for nothing.

Absolutely nothing. Silent tears streamed down her face as she processed all the information. She was so angry, so hurt.

Why had she thought that she could have a happy-ever-after?

Why had she ever believed that Elias loved her?

If he loved her, he would have kept their secret. If he loved her, he would have taken the position. She had been so close to it and it had all been snatched away from her.

There was a knock at the door. It opened and there was Elias.

She glared at him. Angry…so angry with him. She stood up, with her fists clenched.

"What's wrong?" he asked. "Was it bad news about your genetic test?"

"You asshole!" She slapped him hard across the face. Her palm stung. She tried to push past him, but he blocked her exit.

"What was that for?"

"You told Dr. Spiner, who told Dr. Wilder that I was pregnant?" she screamed. "And then you sneak to the hospital to deliver the twins without telling me?"

"I left you a note."

"I didn't see it. You still told people I was pregnant."

He sighed. "I accidentally let it slip to Dr. Spiner and I didn't think that he would say anything. I'm sorry."

She shook her head. "No, you're not. You did this on purpose. All of this."

"I did not," he said angrily. "It was an honest mistake."

"She offered you the position."

"She did, but I turned it down. It should go

to you. I accepted a position here as the chief of the NICU."

"You accepted a position here? In San Francisco?"

"Yes. This is what I want. And I know it's not ideal, with you in San Diego with the baby and me in San Francisco, but…"

Adeline shook her head. "After you turned her down, Dr. Wilder gave it to Dr. Simpson. Dr. Simpson isn't pregnant. I don't have a job."

"Do you really want to work for a woman like that?" Elias asked. "You've done everything for her for a year. You were so focused on her. It made you a brilliant surgeon. You don't need her."

"I do! She's doing research on TTP. I have to be there. Don't you understand? A doctor like her could have saved my mother years of heartache. She could have saved the lives of my sibling."

Elias's expression softened. "I'm sorry that you pinned all those hopes on her, but who's to say you won't discover the cure or the treatment?"

"I won't if I don't learn from her."

"You have learned from her. It's time for you to take a place. You are a competent, well-respected, well-liked surgeon. Why can't you see that?"

She shook her head. "You ruined my chances. I should never have…"

"Should never have slept with me?"

"Right. You broke my trust and for what? You won the position and you're walking away."

"Because I don't need it. I don't want it."

"So you were stringing me along?" Adeline asked sadly. "Obviously you were since you accepted the job here and were planning that I stay in San Diego with our baby!"

"I wanted to tell you."

Adeline wiped the tears away with the back of her hand. "It's a little too late. You tell me to take a leap of faith, but can you? You blame all your problems, all your insecurities on your family. You jump around place to place and are never satisfied. You wanted the position I worked hard for and you earned it, but now you don't want it. Like it's some kind of toy? Just like the baby and I would be some kind of mild distraction to you? What do you want, Elias?"

"I don't… I don't know."

Adeline's heart was crushed. "Well, you're an idiot, Elias Garcia. A complete fool. Congratulations, you won. Which is all I think you cared about in the first place."

Adeline pushed past him.

He didn't try to stop her.

She had to get out of here.

She collected her things and headed outside. She went straight to the apartment and grabbed all her personal belongings. She was going to have to figure out how to get down to San Diego and collect the rest of her stuff, but for now, she knew where to go.

The cab ride didn't take long.

And soon she was in front of her parents' home in Cow Hollow.

She walked up the stairs, exhausted, heartbroken, and not sure what her next steps were going to be. All she could do was ring the doorbell.

There were a few moments before the door opened.

Her mother's eyes widened in surprise. "Adeline? I wasn't expecting you. What are you doing here?"

"I was fired. Can I come in?"

CHAPTER THIRTEEN

ELIAS STOOD THERE.

Crushed.

Why did you let her go?

He didn't know why he had let her walk away. He was scared by her reaction, that she thought him a fool. But she was right about one thing. He jumped around a lot. Never settling, always running away.

Dr. Wilder was crazy not to give the position to Adeline.

He had thought that when he turned it down, she would offer it to Adeline. It was Adeline who deserved it, even though he knew that if Adeline took it, he wouldn't see her and their baby would most likely be raised by him and a nanny. But it was what Adeline wanted.

He had really thought that he was doing the noble thing by turning it down, but it was all for nothing. Adeline hadn't gotten the position and she had walked away from him.

She had walked away from him, just like Shea had.

You walked away from Shea and your family before they did.

And that was a hard thing for him to realize.

You're an idiot, Elias.

What was he so afraid of?

Rejection.

Which was the truth. He was afraid of rejection. He was in love with Adeline and he was greedy. He wanted them to be a family. He wanted them to be a team, and subconsciously, maybe that's why he had told Dr. Spiner that Adeline was pregnant.

He'd made a huge mistake and he had to make things right. He had to find Adeline. He had to win her back.

All he wanted was a relationship with Adeline, but he had been too afraid to reach out and take it.

He had been so afraid of getting hurt again, but really, he was the one who was responsible for everything that had happened in his past.

He was the one who was responsible for his own heartache. When he was with Shea, he had been too focused, too busy trying to distance himself from his family, to prove to them he would be a world-class surgeon, that he was better than working in the family vineyard.

Because he did so, he and Shea had grown

apart. He couldn't blame her for finding solace in a man who was there for her.

He had blamed his heartache on her. Heck, he had blamed all his problems on Shea and Aidan, on his father, because it was easy, because he'd put blinders on to his own faults. He'd been an idiot.

And once again, he was pushing away the woman he loved. The woman who was pregnant with his child, because why? Because he was afraid?

He was afraid of settling down and being happy?

He had to find Adeline and tell her that he was wrong, that he was sorry, and that he loved her. He wanted to be a family. He wanted his child and he would go wherever and do anything if it meant that he could be with Adeline.

Elias left the room and looked around, but there was no sign of Adeline anywhere.

"Dr. Turner left," a nurse said. "She seemed upset."

"Thank you!" Elias quickly went to get his things and ran outside. He ran all the way from the hospital to the apartment, hoping that she was there so he could talk to her. He knew that she was upset with him, but he wondered if she was upset about the results of the genetic testing too. Dr. Wilder had given her the results, but when he had asked her about it, she hadn't answered him.

He needed to talk to her and tell her how he felt.

He needed her forgiveness. And whatever the results of the test were, they could work it out. He wasn't going to leave her. He'd be right by her side the whole time.

He just needed her in his life.

"Adeline?" he called out as he opened the apartment door, but it was eerily quiet and his heart told him that he was too late, that she had left.

He checked her room, but it was empty.

He pulled out his phone and sent a text, asking her where she was, but there was no response.

Come on, Adeline. Let me know you're safe.

She wouldn't answer him. He couldn't stand around here, waiting for her to come back, because he knew she wasn't going to. He knew her parents lived in Cow Hollow, but Cow Hollow was a big section of San Francisco, and Elias was not going to go running up and down the many streets knocking on doors.

It would take too long.

Instead he texted James.

Long story. Adeline didn't get the fellowship. She's missing. Do you know where her parents live?

Now all he had to do was wait, but he couldn't stay here waiting for her.

Instead he left the apartment and made his way down to the rental SUV. He drove to the children's hospital across the city.

He needed to be around his family.

He had to face up to what he'd done to Adeline, and he was tired of running from them, too.

When he got to the children's hospital, he found Aidan wandering around the main lobby with a coffee in his hand.

"Aidan," Elias called out.

Aidan looked up from his phone. "What are you doing here?"

"I came to check on our niece and wanted to make sure that Jeffery had arrived."

Aidan nodded. "He did. Just got here. He's upstairs with Gabrielle in the NICU. They're only allowing one visitor in. I'll be leaving for Napa soon. Shea is coming to get me."

Elias scrubbed his hand over his face. "How is Gabrielle doing?"

"She survived her repair surgery and she should be right as rain. I just got off the phone with Rosa." Aidan grinned. "It's a relief."

"And Rosa is okay?"

"Yes. Adeline saved her life. I know you were just pretending to be engaged to her, but Adeline is a good woman and it's obvious you both care about each other. You'd better snag her before she gets away. You two are made for each other, both strong, hotheaded surgeons."

"Adeline was hardly hotheaded when you saw her briefly," Elias said.

"I heard rumors and you're telling me she's not?" Aidan asked, raising an eyebrow.

"Fine. She's hotheaded."

Aidan cocked his head to the side. "You look wrecked. What happened?"

"I blew it with Adeline. That's what happened." Elias wandered away and sat down in a chair in the main lobby, dropping his head in his hands. "She's gone."

"Gone?" Aidan asked, sitting next to him. "What do you mean gone?"

"She lost the position we were both trying for, and she left, and the reason she didn't get it was my fault."

"How?"

"She's pregnant with my child."

Aidan nodded. "So that's discrimination."

"Yeah, but the doctor in charge laid it all out when we first were applying for the position. Adeline blamed me, because I let it slip that she was pregnant to another doctor and that doctor told our boss. She was angry with me, understandably so, especially when she learned that I turned down the position."

"You turned down the position? Why?" Aidan asked.

"I realized I didn't want it. I wanted to settle down and work here. I wanted to come home and I wanted Adeline with me, but I didn't tell her that. I was afraid she'd reject me. I didn't want to hold her back. Basically, I'm a fool."

"Yeah. I would say so." Aidan sighed. "Look, I know what I did to you was awful. I was jealous of you, you were so smart, and our parents were so proud of you. You had Shea and I was in love with her. You had everything, charm and smarts. I didn't have anything."

"You had something I didn't," Elias said. "You cared for others. I just didn't see it. I thought you hated me. And I thought you were Dad's favorite."

"And I thought you were Dad's favorite." Aidan grinned. "How foolish and stubborn we've been. How so like him we both are."

Elias chuckled. "Great. We're both like Dad. I never hated you, Aidan. For a while I did after Shea, but really, I think I just missed you. I missed my brother."

"I never hated you. I spent time being jealous, thinking you were Dad's favorite. I never saw him being hard on you, only being unfair to me. I missed you too, Elias."

"I've made a right mess of things."

Aidan smiled. "Well, I think we're going to be okay, but with respect to Adeline, you need to make things right with her. It's obvious you both love each other."

Elias cocked an eyebrow. "What?"

"She loves you and if you can't see it, you're blind. I don't know what it is about her, but you're different when you're around her. You need her."

"I would if I knew where she was."

"I thought she was from San Francisco?" Aidan asked. "Do you know where in the city she's from?"

"Cow Hollow."

"Look it up in the phone book."

Elias chuckled. "Who still uses the phone book?"

Aidan rolled his eyes. "Fine, then. Don't find her."

"What do I say?" Elias asked. "How do—I never thought that I would want to get married again. I wanted it, but I was afraid to—I don't know what to say."

"You, the great surgeon, don't know what to say?"

"Right," Elias muttered.

Aidan whacked the top of his head. "You tell her how you feel, you numbskull."

"What if she won't have me? As much as I wasn't there for Shea and I pushed you all away, it still hurt."

"And for that I am sorry, but I don't think Adeline will push you away. She's angry now, but if you go to her, if you tell her how you actually feel, she'll come around. I know she will."

Elias's phone buzzed and he saw a text from James, with an address.

"Did she text you back?"

"No, but now I know where her parents live."

"And you're going to make it right?" Aidan asked.

"I'm going to try." He pocketed his phone. "Give the family my best and wish me luck."

Aidan smiled and nodded. "Good luck. You're going to need it."

"Thanks."

Elias left and drove the rental to Adeline's parents' place in Cow Hollow. He was nervous about laying his heart out there. He wasn't sure if he was going to able to win Adeline over, but he would do everything in his power to win her back, because he knew one thing for certain.

He couldn't live without her.

Adeline was curled up on the couch and her mother brought her a cup of tea. Adeline had cried and all her mother had done was hold her.

Until eventually she stopped crying.

Then her mother went to make the tea and Adeline had finally calmed down.

Her heart was broken, and she realized that it wasn't the job she was mourning, but the loss of her dream. For one brief second, she had thought that she might have it all with Elias, but she had been wrong.

Only this time she really couldn't run from her problems.

She couldn't get away from him like she had from Gregory, because she carried a piece of Elias with her.

"Here, have your tea." Her mother held it out.

"Thanks, Mom."

Her mother took a seat next to her. "Now, what happened that *you*, the surgeon who was recently touted in newspapers, were fired?"

Adeline sighed. "I didn't get that fellowship with Dr. Wilder."

Her mother seemed confused. "Why? You were the front-runner."

"She offered it to someone else."

"That Dr. Garcia?" her mother asked.

"Yes. That Dr. Garcia, who happens to be the father of my baby."

Her mother's eyes widened in surprise. "You're pregnant."

"I am."

Her mother smiled, and then Adeline saw the worry cross her face. "But...your genetic testing."

Adeline pulled out the paper. "It's negative. I don't have the gene, Mom."

Her mother began to cry and smiled. "This is wonderful."

"No, Mom. It's not. The pregnancy is why I

didn't get the position, and because of this baby, I can't… I can't cure TTP."

"You wanted to cure TTP?" her mother asked, surprised.

"Of course I do," Adeline whispered. "How could I not? Mom, it scared me watching you go through that and seeing others go through it. That's why I wanted to get that fellowship."

"You were doing it for me?" her mother asked.

Adeline nodded. "It was all for you and now… now I've lost the position with Dr. Wilder and I won't be able to do it."

"Why ever not?"

"Dr. Wilder offered it to Dr. Garcia. I knew he was trouble when we met a month ago, but I fell for it and he took the position from me." Adeline began to pace. "He took it from me and then he turned it down."

"He turned it down. That doesn't sound like a man who was out to get you. He knows about your child?"

Adeline nodded. "He does, but he made it clear he doesn't want to get married. He said he was going to help with the baby."

"Maybe he turned it down for you?"

Adeline couldn't quite believe it. "That's what he said."

"If the roles were reversed, would you have done the same for him?" her mother asked.

The old her would have said no, but now she wasn't so sure.

"Maybe." Adeline rubbed her temples. "Yes. I love him and I'm happy about the baby."

"You always told me you never wanted a baby."

"I was scared, Mom. I was scared by what happened to you." Tears rolled down her cheeks. "I saw your grief and I know it was because my birth did that to you. I thought that if I could find a cure, it could make up for what I did."

Tears formed in her mother's eyes. "I can't believe you were doing all this for me."

Adeline nodded. "Yes. All for you."

"All I wanted for you was to be happy. That's all I ever wanted. Did you become a doctor just for me? Are you happy with your career?"

Adeline smiled. "I am. I love being a surgeon and I love being an OB-GYN. I love delivering babies, but…now…"

"Now, nothing. You may not have gotten that fellowship, but you are still a qualified surgeon. Just because you didn't get this fellowship with this doctor doesn't mean everything is over. You can still be a surgeon and save lives. You have skills and training and you have a baby on the way. And you can research your own cure if you want. I don't quite understand it all, but you're more than capable of doing your own research, aren't you?"

Her mom was right.

She could.

She'd pinned so much hope on that fellowship, to prove to the world she was the best, but she didn't really care what anyone else thought.

She just cared about Elias.

"I don't have Elias."

"Why not? Have you told him how you feel?"

"No. I'm afraid. What if he rejects me? I don't want to be hurt again."

She wanted her happy-ever-after. She wanted her fairy tale, but she was so scared of her dream shattering again.

Her mother stood and pulled her into an embrace. "You're hurting now. You need to find Elias and make things right."

"What if I can't?"

"Then you know, and you move on." Her mother touched her face. "You need to be strong— you are strong—and you deserve more in life. I love the fact that you wanted to dedicate yourself to solving my problem, because you love me, but you can't live that way. What would make me the happiest would be for you to live the way you want to. You are my child and your happiness is all that matters to me."

"I love you so much, Mom." Adeline held her mother close. "You're going to be an awesome grandma."

"I already am a good grandma. Your twin nephews give me a run for my money most days."

"Right." Adeline hugged her mother again. "I've got to go find Elias. I have to apologize. I've made a huge mistake."

Adeline grabbed her purse and headed for the front door.

She saw that Elias had texted her. She began to text him back when there was a knock at the door. Adeline's heart skipped a beat and she opened it.

Elias was standing there, looking out of breath and exhausted.

He looked as bad as she was feeling.

"Elias, how did you find me?" she asked, stunned.

"Well, at least you're not mad at me anymore."

"No." She sighed. "No. I'm not. I'm sorry."

Elias looked confused. "Sorry for what? I deserved everything I got. I'm sorry I blew your chance with Dr. Wilder."

"There were two of us there in that on-call room, Elias."

"I very much remember that," he said gently.

"You were right. I may not have gotten the position I wanted, but my career isn't over. I'm a surgeon. I've learned a lot from Dr. Wilder, but I was kept as a student for so long that I didn't have the confidence to step up and take what I want. So, thank you for that."

Elias smiled. "You deserved that position, but not at the cost of your own happiness."

"I see that now."

He took her hand in his. "I've realized that I've done some foolish things too. Things that have been detrimental and could potentially threaten my own happiness as well."

Her heart began to race. "What's that?"

"I let you walk away from me." He touched her face. "I love you, Adeline. I was a completely different person when I met you, and that Elias Garcia would have thrown you under the bus to get that position. The problem is, he would have gotten bored and moved on to the next thing because he was trying to prove something to himself. You changed me. I still don't know how. I was so afraid of falling in love again, but I do love you."

Tears stung her eyes. "I love you too."

Elias cupped her face. "I want you to know, Adeline, that I'm willing to go anywhere to be with you. You lead the way. I realized how much I hurt you when I made the decision to take that job here in San Francisco, but I'll give it up. I want you to be happy and I don't want to be apart from you or my child. I want us to be a family."

Her heart soared. "I want that too. And I don't want you to give up your position in San Francisco. I want to stay here too. I was so busy chasing my dreams, focused on curing a genetic disease, that I lost track of why I got into medicine. I wanted to save lives and help women bring new life into the world. Honestly, since we came to San Francisco, I've been happy here. I've been happy leading my own surgeries. I would be happy if we stayed."

"Really?" he asked, smiling.

"Yes. So, if Dr. Spiner still has a position for me, I would like to take it. This is where I belong. I belong here with you."

"Oh, I'm sure that Dr. Spiner still has a position for you. You were the one he originally wanted. When he accidentally let it slip to Dr. Wilder that you were pregnant, he was telling her how he planned to poach you. She was none too pleased."

"Really?" Adeline asked.

"Well, honestly, it's hard to tell with Dr. Wilder. She's a bit of a robot."

"I know."

"We'll be happy here, and I'm sorry for what happened. Please forgive me."

"I'm sorry too." She pulled him in close and kissed him. His arms went around her, and it felt so right. Like it always did. It felt right to be held by him, to have him close. This was where she wanted to be, but she had always been too stubborn to let herself feel it.

She had been too afraid to open her heart and let love in again.

And even though she didn't know what the future held, she wanted to discover that future with Elias and their child.

"Well, now what do we do?" Elias asked. "We're both going to be working in San Francisco. We'll have to go down to San Diego and collect our things."

"We will."

"And we'll have to find a place to stay."

"Yes, we will."

"We could buy a place. I have some money saved away, and given our jobs, it shouldn't be too hard to buy a nice apartment in San Francisco."

"How about a house?" she teased. "We're going to need room for the baby."

He laughed. "Okay. We're going to buy a house. You know that it might be easier for us to buy said house if we were married."

"What?" Adeline asked, stunned.

"I don't have a ring." Elias got down on one knee and held her hand. "Adeline Turner, would you do me the honor of becoming my wife? I love you and I can't picture my crazy life without you."

Adeline smiled and wiped a tear away from her eye. "Yes. Yes, I'll marry you."

Elias grinned and stood, scooping her up in his arms to kiss her. And just as she always did when Elias kissed her, Adeline melted into his arms. Completely lost.

"So, what do we do now?" Adeline said.

"We celebrate. We still have the apartment. Dr. Spiner made it part of my deal. We have it until we can find our own place to live. We could go back there and celebrate?"

"That sounds like a great idea." Her blood was thrumming with desire, thinking about sharing that king-sized bed at the apartment with him.

"I think before you two celebrate, you should introduce my future son-in-law to me."

Adeline laughed and Elias set her on the ground as Adeline's mother came to the doorway.

"Elias, this is my mother, Beverly. Mom, this Dr. Elias Garcia. He's the father of my baby."

"Pleasure is all mine, Mrs. Turner," Elias said, kissing her mother's hand.

Her mother laughed. "I can see why you like him. Well, you might as well come in, Elias. We have some wedding planning to do, and I think you should stay for supper to meet Adeline's father."

"There's no arguing with her. We're going to have to celebrate later," Adeline whispered.

Elias winked at her. "Oh, we will. We have all the time in the world."

And for the first time since Adeline met him, she finally, truly believed him.

She trusted him.

Her heart was whole.

EPILOGUE

Two months later

ADELINE STOOD IN the guest room at the Garcia Estates Vineyard, the one she stayed at often when she and Elias came to visit Flora and Jimeno. In fact, Flora had dubbed it their room.

She was staring at herself in a white wedding dress that had fit a couple of weeks ago and was now decidedly tight.

Adeline frowned. "It had to be twins."

"Twins run in our family," Rosa remarked. "I would have loved to have had twins. Although little Gabrielle here was big enough for twins."

Adeline smiled down at her niece. She was healthy and doing so well two months after her surgery to repair her PDA.

She was fat and happy and dressed in white with a lot of layers of frills.

Adeline hoped that one of her babies was a girl, because she wanted to dress her daughter up in frilly nonsense like that.

252 TWIN SURPRISE FOR THE BABY DOCTOR

"Twins run in our family too," Adeline's mother said from where she was sitting on the bed. "So it's not a surprise that Adeline is carrying twins. My grandsons are twins."

"It was destiny for sure, Beverly," Flora said, coming into the room. "You look so beautiful, Adeline."

"Thank you." Adeline blushed.

"Are they ready for us, Mom?" Rosa asked.

"Yes. I just wanted to come and see the bride." Flora came over and kissed her on the cheek. "Thank you for bringing my son back to me. Welcome to the family."

"Thank you, Flora," Adeline said.

Flora and Rosa left.

It was just her and her mom until her dad came in.

"Well, don't you look absolutely breathtaking." Her father walked over to her and kissed her. "Are you ready for this? Are you sure?"

"Dad, you love Elias. You know I'm ready."

"I just wanted to check." He took her arm and her mother took the other one.

They walked her down the hall and out of the house. The wedding was taking place down in the vineyard, so they walked around the front of the house to where her twin nephews were waiting with the rings.

Gabrielle was the official flower girl, even if

she couldn't walk down the aisle. She was the flower girl by proxy.

The music started and her nephews walked ahead.

Her heart was hammering. She was nervous, but this was the best thing she was ever going to do, and she was ready to be married to Elias and spend the rest of her life with him.

She had never thought a few months ago that she would be here. On her wedding day and pregnant with twins.

Her parents were smiling as they walked down the garden path to the wooden arch that Jimeno had made for them.

Tears stung in her eyes when she saw Elias at the end of the aisle in his tuxedo, with his best man, Manny, by his side.

"Ladies and gentlemen, please stand for the bride," the minister said.

Everyone stood up, and as she walked down that aisle, she saw everyone who had supported her. Her family and her friends, including James and Sherrie.

Staff from the hospital in San Francisco where they worked.

And even Dr. Wilder, who smiled and nodded as she walked by.

Elias hadn't wanted to invite her, but it was because of Dr. Wilder that she had met the love of her life, and Adeline had spent so many years with her, it felt right that she was there.

They stopped at the end of the aisle and her parents turned to her, kissing her.

"Who gives this woman to be wed to this man?"

"Her mother and I do," her father said, his voice catching.

"You may be seated," the minister said.

Elias stepped closer and took her hands, which were trembling.

"You look beautiful," he whispered.

"Thank you. You look so handsome."

"No one is looking at me."

Adeline's heart skipped a beat. All she could do was stare at this man who had changed her life for the better. She knew she had changed his life for the better too. They were a dream team in so many ways.

Their practice in San Francisco was already flourishing after a couple of months. People flocked to see her and to see Elias. The NICU at the Hospital for Special Surgery in San Francisco was being revamped thanks to an influx of money that they had brought in.

So they could save more lives.

They had never been happier. Things would be difficult with the twins coming and they would be busy, but they could make it work.

They were a team.

She looked out at all the people in their lives,
without whom this moment wouldn't have been
possible. Without whom this moment between
her and Elias would never have happened.

And she finally understood it all.

She knew that she'd made the right decision.
Her instincts were telling her that this was right,
and this was the path she was supposed to take.

Every painful moment had brought her here
and she wouldn't change a thing. Except she
wished she had found Elias sooner.

"Do you, Elias Alejandro Garcia, take Adeline Victoria Turner to be your lawfully wed-
ded wife?"

"I do." Elias slipped the ring on her finger.

"And do you, Adeline Victoria Turner, take
Elias Alejandro Garcia to be your lawfully wed-
ded husband?"

"I do." And she took the ring from her nephew
and slipped it on his finger.

"Then, by the powers vested in me by the state
of California, I now pronounce you man and wife.
You may kiss your bride."

Everyone cheered as Elias lifted the veil and
kissed her. And the moment his lips touched hers,
there was a flutter and she gasped.

"What?" asked Elias over the noise of everyone cheering.

"The babies. The quickening." Tears slid down

her cheeks. "I guess they wanted to be a part of today too."

Elias grinned and touched her belly. Although he knew he couldn't feel the babies, they moved under his hand, as if they knew their father was there.

"I love you, Adeline." Elias kissed her hand.

"I love you too. Now, let's walk down the aisle and start the rest of our lives."

"Your wish is my command, Mrs. Garcia."

She nudged him. "That's Dr. Garcia."

Elias laughed and took her hand. They ran down the aisle being pelted with flower petals by the people who meant the most to them.

In the place where they had found their happily-ever-after.

* * * * *

If you enjoyed this story, check out these other great reads from Amy Ruttan

A Reunion, a Wedding, a Family
Reunited with Her Hot-Shot Surgeon
Baby Bombshell for the Doctor Prince
Pregnant with the Paramedic's Baby

All available now!